CRYSTAL LAKE ENTERTAINMENT PRESENTS
MEMENTO MORI INK MAGAZINE
© 2024

www.crystallakepub.com
www.memento-mori.ink

ISBN 978-1-964398-16-7

WE ARE DARKNESS
COME AND PLAY
WITH US

CRYSTAL LAKE PRESENTS

MEMENTO MORI INK

Can you disappear so completely that only one person remembers you existed?

That's what comics creator Linda Corrigan asks, when her editor, disappears without a trace. Drawn into an FBI investigation by Agent McPherson, Linda and comics historian Richard Ford unearth a chilling link to the forgotten comic artist R.L. Carver, whose work might just hold the key to a series of mysterious disappearances.

As they explore Carver's life, they uncover the secret history of horror comics, the misfits, madcaps and macabre masters who forged an industry, frightened a generation and felt the heat of the Federal Government. They also stumble on the shadow history of the United States on a road trip that veers into the nation's dark underbelly, where forbidden knowledge and forgotten lore await them.

THE SECRET HISTORY OF HORROR COMICS THREATENS TO UNLOCK THE SHADOW HISTORY OF THE UNITED STATES.

Crystal Lake's Dark Tide series

TABLE OF CONTENTS

Cover art by Abstract Photography

Cover model is Primal

There is nothing that feels as good as coming out of isolation, even for someone who builds their own fortress around themselves. Knowing there is someone who understands the purpose of art, who relates to how it can fill a void, and who knows the depth of how it heals is like curling up in a warm blanket.

Creating a family from this vision is a dark blessing.

This community, like all communities, can be cold and toxic. At the end of the day, knowing there is a *home* to go to that provides shelter from demons we fight all our life is a once-in-a-lifetime occurrence.

We've created it here.

It started with House of Stitched, and it evolved to Memento Mori Ink. The pride and passion of what we do is evident in every page you'll indulge in. It is our vulnerability, it is our heart, and it is our soul, laid out bare before your eyes.

We hope you enjoy it, and most of all, we hope you share the word because there are others like us who *need* this space of acceptance and safety.

This place is safe for everyone, from all walks of life, who know what it is like to be shunned for being a "little different." Or maybe a lot different.

But I digress.

Memento Mori Ink is here because there is a strong need for behind-the-scenes adventures into darkness with experienced guides who can escort us through its labyrinthine and treacherous paths.

This is a kingdom built from shadows and shrouded in mystery. Beneath the eternal midnight sun, we play with nocturnal creatures and tell stories to keep the *real* monsters at bay.

We welcome you, weary traveler, into its sanctum for as long as you wish to stay, so long as you respect three rules:

1. Be *You*, authentically.
2. *Respect* the others who you'll find here.
3. Leave a wish in the Moonlight Well.

Forever in Darkness,

Welcome to the first issue of Memento Mori Ink Magazine. As your curator for the content within, I would like to offer this slice of information to use as breadcrumbs on your journey.

For this issue, I posed a theme to the writers and creators, and I told them to interpret it how they would. I love to give a concept and see how artists will translate the information and then return it. It's what this magazine is all about— the process and manifesting of ideas into the end result.

Allow me to introduce our freelance columnists and their MONSTERS INSIDE.

The Madness Within

Sam Gregory

No twist in horror comes as a bigger surprise than finding out one of the "good" guys is actually the bad guy. A popular trope, it has been used many times and, if done right, can genuinely shock an audience. This character we have been watching that we might actually care about is suddenly revealed to be the killer, turning everything on its head.

One of the most famous examples is Norman Bates in *Psycho*. While something of an oddball, we are led to believe his mother is the killer, when in reality, Norman is posing as her to attack his victims. For most of the movie, he comes across as quite mild mannered and timid. It is only later that we see the cracks in his facade. Madness cannot be hidden for long. When he utters the famous line, "We all go a little mad sometimes," you can see a hint of that madness in his eyes, leaving viewers very unsettled. The line was echoed in the '90s hit *Scream*, where the double twist revealed that the main character's boyfriend was the killer, along with his best friend. In both these movies, mothers seemed to be the motivation for their madness too.

Speaking of mad mothers, who can forget Mrs. Voorhees from *Friday the 13th*. As the bodies of teenage camp counsellors start to pile up, she is a seemingly nice woman who wants to help them. The reality is she is a woman driven mad by the death of her son. Here, the roles are similar to *Psycho* but reversed, with Mrs. Voorhees hearing her son's voice urging her to kill. The movie spawned an entire series, switching killers by reviving Jason Voorhees after his mother was murdered. While this did change the dynamic—no one would believe that Jason was innocent—it did spawn many sequels.

The idea that someone can seem innocent on the outside while having this darkness within them makes for great storytelling. Especially when you set your audience up to believe it is anyone but them. The twist works particularly well on female killers or characters who are perceived as weak in some way.

In real life, we face a similar issue. Who hasn't met someone who seemed nice on the surface but then showed their true colors later? Yet many people believe that what you see is what you get. Too often, we are fooled by a few kind words or a friendly face. We can never know what is going on inside someone's head, though. Perhaps that would be the truly frightening thing—to hear their inner thoughts and know what they really think of us.

But does this trope still work today? Yes and no. In the past, movies featured characters with mental health issues that were grossly exaggerated or did not match the actual condition. Often, these characters were seen as violent, when in reality, that is rarely the case with certain conditions. We have come a long way, and more care is taken to portray these conditions as accurately as possible in order to prevent stigma. If using a similar trope today, it is important to do thorough research into mental health conditions and how it affects the individual. Of course, you could go the generic route and claim your killer is simply "mad" without the specifics.

Horror goes through cycles, with various tropes being popular at different times, depending on current events and what new fears they bring. In the '80s, we had killer dolls, while today these dolls have evolved to be controlled by AI. The monsters may change, but one thing that does not change is our inability to truly know a person. In real life too, how many of us wear "masks" every day? The faces we show to one another in public are not the same as the ones we have in private. We all do it to some degree; some people are just more deceptive than others. This is why this trope remains popular. Readers and moviegoers gain a special insight and get to see that private face, that glimpse into a person that others may not. That part of them they want to keep hidden.

But madness rarely stays hidden for long.

The Monster Inside

Z. Martin

You long to see the monster waiting inside the person walking down the street. Don't you? Come on, we all do. That's why 62% of Americans watch social media surrounding serial killers.

Why else would we as a society be so obsessed with them? The people that look so normal on the outside. The people that hold in their demons until they no longer can. How well do you know the person passing you on the street?

Let's really think about that for a moment. How well do you know the person next to you? The person you just passed by? The person that delivered your pizza yesterday? Do we really know these people?

What monsters hide within them? Is it depression, anxiety, suicidal tendencies, or a laundry list of other diagnoses? Have your attention now, don't I?

We often go through our daily lives focused on ourselves and our immediate family. So often so that we never see the monsters lurking within the people we interact with. The fact of the matter is 1 in 10 people have depression, while 1 in 3 have anxiety, and over 50,000 people committed suicide in 2023 in the United States.

With these alarming numbers staring you in the face, ask yourself now: How well do I know the person next to me? What monster is latched on to their back? What demon is gnawing away at their gray matter?

This is something I can speak personally on. I am a 34-year-old male at the time of writing this. I went through 33 years of my life believing that how I felt in my head was normal. I fully thought I was supposed to get nervous every time someone wanted to talk to me. I thought a racing heart, sweaty palms, and rage were normal while shopping. Until I finally spoke up for myself.

I marched into my doctor's office and demanded they fix me! Well, not really. In actuality, I made an appointment and spoke with my doctor over my concerns. Being the lovely doctor she is, she prescribed me some medication, and after some tweaking, we got it right.

I no longer jump out of my skin over a phone call. I don't get rage just from stepping into a packed store. Most importantly, I'm better with my wife and kids. I'm happier than I've ever been in my 34 years of life, and it reflects onto my family. Another tidbit of information on this: I was in the United States Marine Corps for 8 years.

Why did I say that last part? Well, it's simple, really. I know many of my brothers and sisters in the armed forces don't believe they need medicine to live healthy. I'm here to tell you that you're wrong. You have to talk to someone who will listen.

I went through my life wearing a mask. A mask that showed people I was happy and functioning while inside I was screaming. The monster inside me ate away at me piece by piece, day after day. It's okay to put the mask away for a while and address what's making you wear it.

I say all of this in hopes that this will slightly alter your perception. You can't always see the monster inside someone. Sometimes, people are crying out for help in their own way, and you can't decipher it. Look beyond the mask. Hear those whispered screams.

Open your mind, ears, eyes, and hearts. That's the only way to rid people of the monsters inside.

Art, the Monster of the Creator into the Mind of the Author of *Muse*

Jacque Day

In her debut novella, *Muse*, LCW Allingham unites art and horror in a dark tale of the genius behind raw talent and the cost of consuming it.

From their Fifth-Avenue brownstone, the associates wield a mysterious power over the New York art world. Mr. Black, a charismatic art critic, uses his influence to manipulate, charm, and control. Benefactor and financier Mr. Silver lavishes artists with parties and luxurious apartments, but his true desire is to possess the creators and their work. Mr. Green finds and nurtures talent. Together, they weave an impenetrable—so they believe—web, snaring artists with exceptional raw talent and consuming them until all that remains is a husk.

Now, the well has run dry. The associates need new blood.

They're hungry.

Mr. Black declares, "Glonciel is done, dried up." With this, he touches off a litany of disappointments in their present stable of artists—notably, former street tagger Malik Jackson; Cedric Fleck, who works in pastels; and Dana Glonciel, a mere shadow of her former self. Mr. Green meagerly attempts to argue for the artists' merits, pleading, "If you would only give them a chance." But he caves and sets out to meet their demands.

It is in this place, this moment of crisis for the associates, that LCW Allingham slips into the world of her new horror novella, *Muse*.

As a basis for the story, Allingham draws on the very real horror of artist burnout. "The way that so many artists have burned themselves out trying to create, trying to expel their daemons or their genius through painting," she says. "There's nothing worse than having it in you and not being able to do it, not being able to get it all out." Thus, the potential for art to destroy the creator runs very near the surface of her consciousness.

"Every piece of art is a monster of the creator."

For the author, the topic of art consuming its creator hits close to home.

As she reflects on this, Allingham, who goes by the informal LC, sits on her sofa. On the wall behind her hangs a gallery spanning three generations of family creativity. At the uppermost left is a painting by her late mother, Patricia Allingham Carlson, a career artist and art teacher. In the upper right hangs a painting by LC's grandmother, Claire Carlson. Between them is a painting LC started during COVID and hasn't yet completed.

Growing up in suburban Philadelphia surrounded by artists, craftspeople, and musicians, LC recalls animated family discussions about "how art in any form can elevate you or destroy you as the artist."

The concept of art as something that possesses the creator—as daemon, genius, or muse—was a common theme in LC's discussions with her mother. "I wonder if creativity isn't some kind of chemical reaction," she says, "where you have this raw inspiration coming to you from the muses, and it has to be mixed with what you have, the deep, dark, inner parts of your soul in order to make it special. I talked to my mom about this all the time, and we both very much felt like it comes from outside and it moves through you."

Does a talent for art, the nose for it, the desire for it, live in the blood? Does the appetite for art exist at the primal level, rooted in the DNA? If you passed a descendant of seventeenth-century Dutch painter Johannes Vermeer on the streets of New York today, would you know it?

Is anyone, at all, what they seem?

Muse challenges the very core of these questions.

In his nationwide quest for new talent, Mr. Green is seated at a bus terminal in the middle of nowhere when he overhears a "neo-hipster punk" talking about a trailer park-dwelling welder who carts around art supplies, not for himself but for his neighbor. Mr. Green makes an inquiry and learns that the welder, whose name is Jim, lives in a double-wide next door to Terra Desmarais. When Mr. Green steps into Terra's trailer, he discovers a collection of art the likes of which he has never seen.

He has found the next new thing. He takes Terra to New York and unleashes her on the world.

Quietly, he begins to feed.

But the cost, the associates discover, is far more than they bargained for.

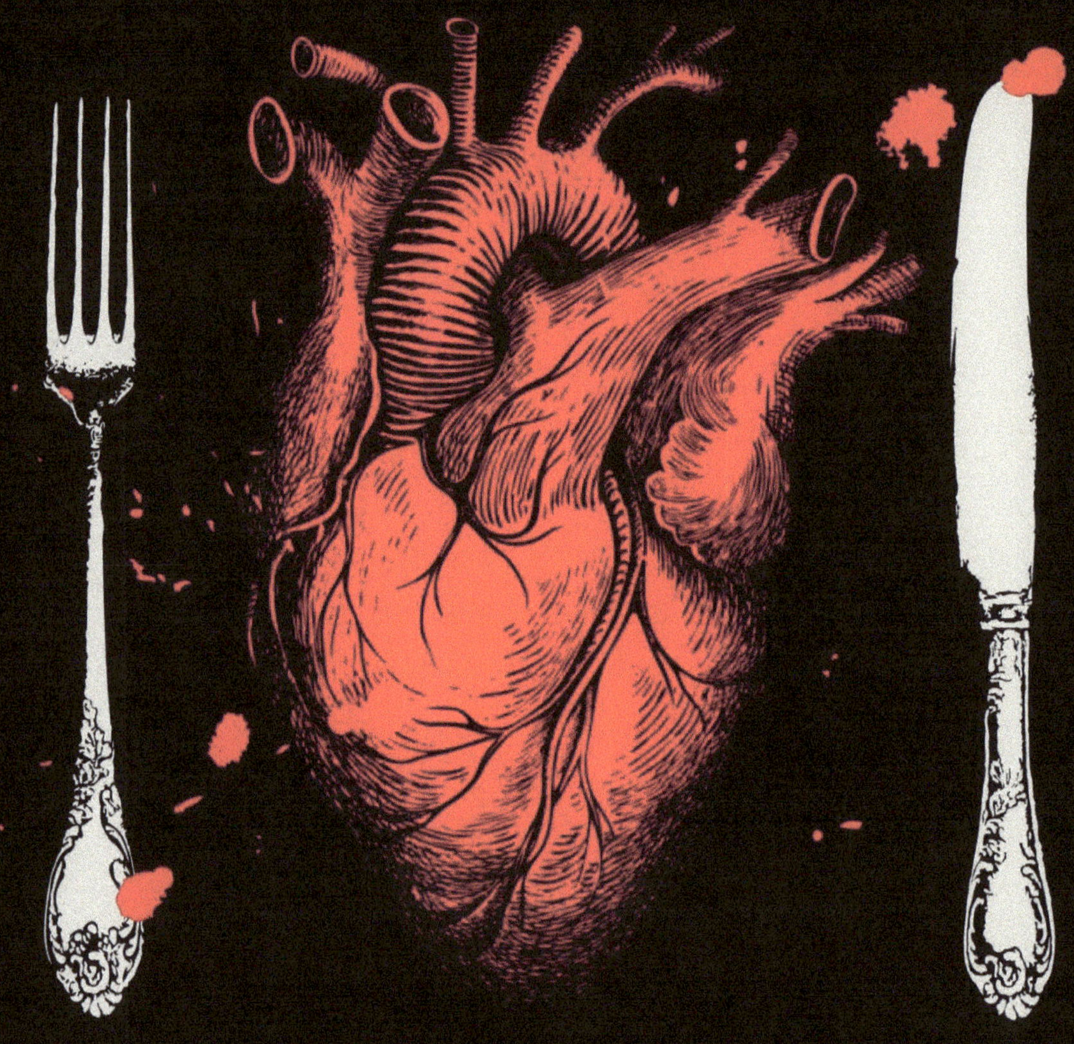

THE CURIOUS CUISINE PENCHANT OF ISSEI SAGAWA

BY JAE MAZER

As authors, we all look for ways to boost our sales. In a day and age where social media and viral videos are a path to success, many creatives try different strategies to garner attention online. In recent times, we have seen authors fake illness for attention, engage in vicious yet entertaining feuds with other authors, and some have even gone as far as burning their own books and claiming it was someone else in order to stir on controversy that brings them attention they are so desperate to attain.

Issei Sagawa gained notoriety and best-seller status because of controversy he drummed up unintentionally. In this case, however, it wasn't as simple as book burning or vitriol spitting.

Issei Sagawa graduated with a master's degree in English Literature from Kwansei Gakuin University and was pursuing a PhD in Literature at the Sorbonne in Paris, France, when his life took an expected turn. After moving from Paris back to Japan, he became a best-selling author who published eighteen books, wrote restaurant reviews for the Japanese magazine *Spa*, and published articles and stories in a number of journals.

Did he ever receive his PhD? No, he did not. Why did he move from Paris before completing his degree? Well, he didn't quite move. He was deported for murder and cannibalism.

In 1981, Sagawa shot and killed his classmate, Dutch student Renee Hartevelt, because he wanted to eat her. He stated later that he didn't really want to kill her, he only meant to eat her.

"**What I truly wished was to eat her living flesh. Nobody believes me, but my ultimate intention was to eat her, not necessarily to kill her ... If only she'd let me taste her a little bit." (Kaonga, 2022).**

After shooting Hartevelt during dinner at his apartment, he raped her corpse, cut her up, and froze pieces of her to cook and consume at his leisure. He put the parts of her he didn't use in a suitcase and was going to dispose of the suitcase in the water in The Bois de Boulogne Park, but a passerby found it odd that the suitcase was dripping blood and contacted the authorities. Sagawa was subsequently arrested.

A psychiatric evaluation determined that Sagawa was insane and unfit to stand trial, so he was placed in a mental institution before his deportation to Japan. Once back on Japanese soil, Sagawa's mental health was reevaluated. This time, the doctors found that Sagawa was mentally competent, and the justice system intended on putting him on trial for his crimes in France. However, because the case in France was closed at the time of deportation, all evidence had already been disposed of. The Japanese authorities, having nothing concrete to go to trial with, were forced to allow Sagawa to go free.

Thus begins the story of Issei Sagawa, best-selling author and columnist. After he was freed of this whole ordeal, Sagawa wrote his novel *In the Fog*—a memoir that described his lifelong lust for human meat, a detailed account of the murder, rape, and consumption of Hartevelt, and numerous other incidents in his life where he would hire prostitutes almost every night with the intention of shooting and eating them but could never quite pull the trigger. *In the Fog*—and his other titles, including a graphic manga that dealt with murder and cannibalism—skyrocketed Sagawa to celebrity status, earning him monikers such as "The Kobe Cannibal."

Issei Sagawa passed away a free man and best-selling author at the age of seventy-three, when he succumbed to pneumonia on November 24, 2022. I have to wonder if he ever did get his wish, which he expressed more than once in the years before his death, including in his memoir: to taste human meat one more time before he died.

Scott, M. David. "10 Fiction Authors Who Committed Very Real Crimes." *Society, July 08th, 2019.*

https://listverse.com/2019/07/08/10-fiction-authors-who-committed-very-real-crimes/

Kaonga, Gerard. "Issei Sagawa Dead: Why Notorious Cannibal Killer Never Saw Jail." *Newsweek*. Published Dec 02, 2022 at 7:21 AM EST.

Morris, Steven (20 September 2007). "Issei Sagawa: Celebrity Cannibal". *New Criminologist*. Archived from the original on 14 July 2011.

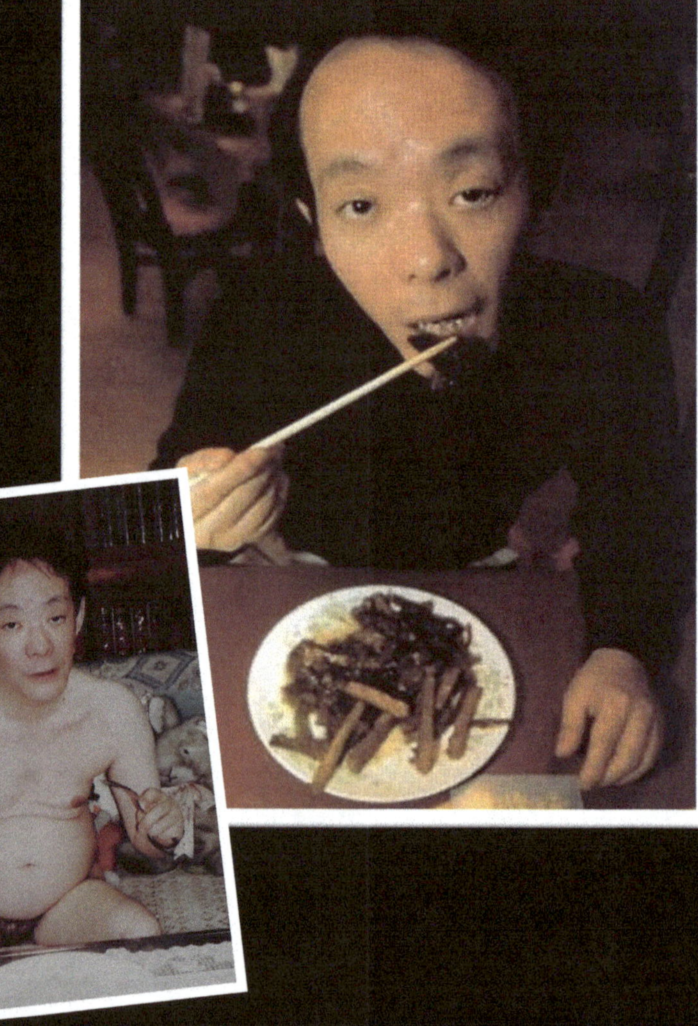

BOOKS OF HORROR
PRESENTS
BOOKS & BREWS
DOUBLE CLUTCH BREWING COMPANY
EVANSTON, ILLINOIS
AUGUST 3, 2024

GAGE GREENWOOD
WINTER'S MYTHS
SEASON ONE

INCIDENTS
AROUND
THE
HOUSE
JOSH
MALERMAN

A ROCK N' ROLL NOVEL
ATOMIC LOVE
A HEAVY METAL MEMOIR
The sex, dirt and blood of rock n' roll.
JESSIE ROSE

LISA BREANNE

BEN YOUNG

THE
TERROR
OF
WILLOW
FALLS
AN EVENTIER NOVEL
JAY BOWER

NECRONADO
RJ ROLES

MATTHEW LUTTON

Greetings, readers, gamers, and dwellers of the dark. I bring to you a hidden gem of a game that deserves much more attention than it gets. I recommend that everyone give this game a try, despite its cruel and unforgiving nature. Whether you're a fan of grim and Lovecraftian horror or looking for a challenging yet rewarding turn-based rogue-like game, *Darkest Dungeon II* is for you.

I want to clarify that this game can be *BRUTALLY* difficult. The game even tells you upon launch: "It's about making the best of a bad situation." Even when things seem dire, stick it out and fight to the end (unless you're on the third battle and have lost three of your four party members). No matter the situation you find yourself in, perseverance is key. Keep cool, analyze your options, and you might just barely make it out with your team intact. Another thing that I want to establish is that I have not fully beaten this game. Yes, it's *that* hard. Even the item specifically given to make the game easier only gives you the slightest edge. Still think you can brave the *Darkest Dungeon II*? Then let's get into it!

Oddly enough, *Darkest Dungeon II* doesn't really have an in-depth story. It's mainly told through very vague dialogue moments before the start of every run. Each level reveals a small portion of the larger backstory to the game. The entire game is a point-of-view from the player, narrated through a character known as "the Teacher."

A prologue reveals that he is your mentor and friend. The two of you were studying the occult before an experiment triggered a catastrophe that unleashed madness upon the world. The Teacher (voiced by Wayne June) gives you a spark of light, which he calls "Hope." However, it is the very last of its kind. You, his "Protégé," must brave the horrors that ravage the world with it in a desperate attempt to avert the coming apocalypse. Although, there seems to be more to this story than what is let on . . .

That's about all you're given story-wise. The rest is fed to you in chunks as you complete the different acts in the game. Speaking of, let's get into the gameplay.

Darkest Dungeon II plays like a JRPG (Japanese roleplaying game), where the turns are based on your character's speed stat. Instead of one side taking their turn before moving to the other, one character takes their turn, and depending on an ally/enemy's speed stat, goes next after them. This can be either an ally or an enemy, which spices things up a bit and really makes you think about your tactics. When the game starts, you pick an "Act," which measures the length, difficulty, and the types of enemies you will face on your journey. Next is "the Crossroads," where you will select your heroes for the upcoming journey.

The game allows you to select four characters that form your party. Each one has their own unique playstyle and abilities. Mix and match to see which ones synergize with each other. Do beware, however. As your journey progresses, certain actions and decisions cause your party members' relationships to strengthen or wain. Depending on the outcome, using specific abilities could cause buffs or debuffs, or even make your heroes turn on each other. When forming your team, be careful with your composition, as this also affects their relations. After selecting your heroes, the harrowing trek to the Mountain begins, where the final boss of each act lies in wait . . .

Throughout the path to the Mountain, you will face all manner of beings, from undead to pyromaniac cultists or even horrific creatures from the void. As you progress through the run, you can select which path you wish to take. Some will lead you to artifacts that grant your party members buffs, or to refugees seeking assistance by the roadside. Every decision counts, whether it be in combat or travel. With each encounter, some of your party members will build up a debuff called "stress" (relatable). If your character reaches 10 stacks of stress, it causes one of two events to happen where that party member either stays "Resolute" in themselves, regaining full health and resetting the stress bar, or they could have a "Meltdown" and lose all but a small portion of their health as well as cause the other party members to gain stress. Stress, if not managed properly, can prove catastrophic for your run. And, by the way, if you fail a run, your progress is reset. This adds to the challenging and brutal nature of this game.

Each act has a set amount of levels. At the end of every level, you reach "the Inn", a place of rest and respite for your characters. Here, you can buy trinkets, use certain items, enhance your characters' abilities, or mount your stagecoach with items that could prove beneficial for your journey. Make sure to use your time here wisely! Once you feel you're prepared enough to continue, select the next level and press on to the Mountain.

Combat in *Darkest Dungeon II* can be… I'll be honest, a little bullshit. In some encounters, if played correctly, you absolutely wipe the floor with your enemy. However, in most others the game will decide that every enemy will hit you for a 27 damage crit, applying bleed and burn as well as skipping your character's next turn. Things like that sometimes turn a promising run into a complete wash. Even if you make it to the Inn with one member left, you can replace your dead heroes with others. Though that just takes the point out of your whole team composition, right? While that may be true, remember, it's about making the best of a bad situation. You *could* give up and reset the run, but I find that pushing through with your new party proves surprisingly rewarding. Always weigh your options carefully.

Whether you make it to the Mountain and defeat the boss or perish along the way, the game rewards you with "candles." This currency persists through your journeys and can be used to make your characters a little better permanently, have different items and trinkets appear, or even get some cosmetics to give your heroes some personality—flair is important when stopping the apocalypse from happening. After spending your candles, it's time to begin another run!

The more you play through *Darkest Dungeon II*, the more you'll start to learn, like which characters synergize best with each other or what team comp works with the type of playstyle you're looking for! Each failure yields results no matter what. Never stop trying new things along your journey. Even if you find a team comp you really like, experiment with new ones!

In conclusion, I find that *Darkest Dungeon II* earns an 8 out of 10 from me. The aesthetic is haunting yet beautifully well done, and the gameplay is rewarding to those who truly stick it out. Unfortunately, the lack of any *real* story being told until later levels (which are hard enough to unlock as it is), combined with sudden difficulty spikes, takes off a couple points, in my opinion. However, I still strongly recommend that you give it a try and play through it a few times! Even if you don't completely finish the game, it's still a satisfying, incredible, and fun experience.

Darkest Dungeon II was developed and published by Red Hook Studios and released May 8, 2023. It has overall "Mostly Positive" reviews on Steam as of the writing this article.

Thank you so much for reading, and I hope to bring you another game review soon!

Cameron Fuller is a serious gamer who is also passionate about acting, cooking, and photography. In his spare time, you can find him unleashing his sharpened wit on (E) Trolls.

THE CHARACTERS

Varek

Red Varek

Cyrus

Leviathan

Bone Daddy

Horde

Decimus

Ingolfur

Crossroads Demon

Alpha

Omega

PRIMAL
BIGGER AND BADDER

"I want to tell you a little story," his voice rumbled in the darkness. I squinted my eyes but could not penetrate the thickness of it. For now, he was a faceless entity enveloping me in a shroud of fear.

"Please don't hurt me," I said. My voice quivered, betraying years of buried trauma resurfacing in the presence of this unknown threat. I cursed myself in silence for the childhood fear still haunting me, tightening my chest in this moment of vulnerability.

The body will respond to danger in the most primal way. It starts with a rush of adrenaline. Like a drug, it gets pushed through dilated veins and jacks up your heart until you can feel yourself running in place even though you're frozen in place.

I stood there. My muscles became rigid and unmoving. Until his breath caressed the back of my neck, rewriting the air around me like a cold finger of Death dragging my soul down the length of my spine.

My brain exploded with a chaotic symphony of fear and adrenaline, each note reminding me of past encounters with danger. Amidst the terror, an unsettling wave of euphoria washed over me — a perverse recognition that, in these moments, I felt more alive than ever.

In moments like this, some humans experience a strange phenomenon psychologists call "benign masochism." It's the brain's peculiar way of turning fear and even pain into a twisted sort of pleasure. I wasn't sure if it was the rush of adrenaline or some deeper psychological twist that made me almost crave the terror, but amidst the fear, there was an odd sense of exhilaration, like dancing on the edge of a knife.

Tears welled in my eyes and looked up to fight them knowing once they came, I would feel relief, a spiritual cleansing, and yes, a sense of sexual gratification.

I could feel the air particles move behind me as he closed in, brushing lips across the shell of my ear in prelude to the tightening of his hand around my neck. The air to my overworking lungs was being cut off by the strength of the grip.

"You're not listening," he growled.

And then, all at once, I was. Every single fiber of my being was listening. My skin prickled to attention, my heart battered through my ribcage in a race to be closer to him, and my body melted against his solid frame.

The tears won. Streams of them trailed down my cheeks like raindrops chasing each other to the bottom of the window.

"I've chased you long enough through dreams," he continued. "You called for me, and now I'm here."

His fingers tightened again and the air I was pulling into my lungs began to wheeze and stars were filling my eyes with bursts of color against the black void.

I tried to open my mouth to speak but the words were cut off by the impact of my body being thrown against the wall. Before I could scream, the demon's body pressed against mine. If you've never felt the weight of a truck resting on your chest, I can never put it into words enough for you to understand.

He pressed in, slow. He *wanted* me to feel the panic rise as consciousness slipped from me. Through the burst of stars, he leaned in and I could finally see the glow of his smile. His eyes, dark as oil, mirrored my terror and I watched my soul exiting my body.

"Now," he whispered with a hint of amusement. "Let me in, and I'll let you live."

Photos by Charlie Pierce of Abztract Photo

SARA WINDSCHITL

ARACHNID ARCHITECT

Lisa Vasquez: Tell us a bit about you and how you got into creating these amazing enclosures!

Sara Windschitl: Sure! My name is Sara, and I've always been artistic. As far back as I remember, I was always drawing or creating things from various mediums, etc. [*laughs*] I have a very active imagination, so I decided in 2017 to start my business and put that imagination and those ideas to use. About the enclosures, in 2021, I found my first two jumping spiders (some adorable Bolds). Shortly after that (in December), I wanted to create for them enclosures that provide lots of textures and things for them to explore, as jumping spiders are curious by nature. I posted them to social media, and people started asking if I sell them. That's how my enclosures came to be. [*smiles*] Last year, I decided to expand into miniatures and add those in (I create 98% of my decor from scratch) to not only make the enclosures fun and enjoyable for the owner but for the spiders as well. Plus, the enclosures double as display pieces. [*laughs*]

LV: What's the craziest request you've received so far?

SW: Oh, there's been a few [*laughs*]. Not so much crazy as interesting! I've had requests for enclosures for stick bugs, all the way up to "adult" themed enclosures [*laughs*]. I'll be creating a greenhouse enclosure for an Orchid mantis here soon!

LV: I know you put a lot of hours and passion into your work. How do you come up with new ideas?

SW: It's funny, but usually, the ideas come on a whim [*laughs*]. I will look at the enclosure or a decor piece, and my imagination just starts creating designs and mentally placing things in the enclosure [*laughs*]. If I have the pieces in my possession, I'll just start placing them until I feel it looks good. Or I've also had ideas for designs present to me in dreams [*laughs*].

LV: As a small business, how do you handle having to do your own marketing, do the creating and shopping, and taking orders? Was it something that came naturally, or was there some trial and error?

SW: There was definitely some trial and error [*laughs*]. But it's literally a daily job, with long hours and no days off. I'm always doing something for the business, whether it's marketing on social media, working on the orders, or shopping for supplies.

LV: What has been the hardest part of what you do?

SW: I'd say the hardest part is balancing the business aspect with my personal life. As I said, I really don't get days off, as I'm always doing something. I also have some health issues that I deal with daily, and at times, those slow down my ability to work quickly on my orders and such.

LV: Have you taken inspiration from somewhere? If so, who or what?

SW: I'd say my biggest inspiration in enclosure making is a combo of a person, who is my friend Brittany Bush of Spood Manor (literally the OG), and my love of fantasy—such as Lord of the Rings, Game of Thrones—and rustic cabins/cottages and the nature around me. I've grown in my art to now have my own aesthetic where my enclosures are concerned. [*smiles*]

LV: With your inspiration, you still want to put your own signature in your work. How do you spin your style into every piece?

SW: I try to stay "true" to my ideas and such. I tend to have a more rustic/fantasy vibe, and that shows in my art. It's so amazing when someone looks at a picture of my enclosures and knows that it's my design before they see the watermark I add to each photo [*laughs*] .

LV: Which piece is your favorite and why?

SW: It's so hard to choose [*laughs*]! I have so many, to be honest; recently, it is the Apothecary one I created as a custom, and the current "deluxe" version of my Three Spiders Shoppe that I'm creating for a good friend.

LV: What bit of information, if you knew when you started, would've changed everything for you?

SW: It's not so much outside info as inside info. I would be more confident in my abilities and my art [*laughs*]. I sometimes find myself doubting my art, and that can actually be detrimental to your artistic process, evolution, and your business. When you doubt yourself, it reflects in your work.

LV: Tell us where you find you amazing creations!

SW: I have my Etsy, which is https://www.etsy.com/shop/WolfSpiritArtsby Sara

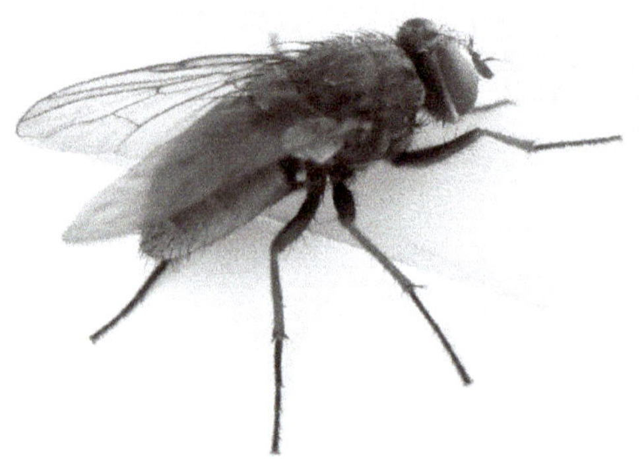

Wolf Spirit Arts by Sara
© 2024

CHOCOLATIER
Handmade Chocolate
Desserts
Welcome to our chocolate shop.
welcome

THE APOTHECARY
TARANTULA
CRIBS

Wolf Spirit Arts by Sara
© 2024
DEATH
OMENS
Alchemy
Necromancy
TARANTULA

MEMENTO
MORI
INK

SWAG

HOOK
OF
RELATIBILITY
BY AJ BROWN

Picture this:

There's a man sitting on a park bench. He wears dark brown slacks, maybe even bordering on black. His shirt is nothing more than a tan button-down with light brown vertical stripes. He wears dirty sneakers with frayed, once white shoelaces tied into haphazard bows. He's older, mid-seventies, maybe early eighties, bald except for a ring of white hair that forms a C from the back of one ear to the back of the other one. A scrim of sweat clings to his forehead. In one hand is a plastic bag full of broken pieces of bread. The other hand is tossing some of those pieces onto the red brick path in front of him. There are weeds growing between the cracks of those bricks, little pieces of green no one really pays attention to. Gray and white pigeons peck at the bricks, plucking pieces of bread up in their beaks.

The man looks away from the pigeons and the lonely sidewalk, the bread crumbs still there, and up to the blue sky. Gray and black clouds hang off in the distance, threatening a storm, or at the very least, rain. Still, the sun is bright and warm on his skin. He should have put some lotion on his bald head to protect it. Lillian would have made sure he did that. He takes a deep breath. Tears form in his eyes. When they fall, they mix with sweat. No one would be able to tell anything was wrong unless they look hard at his red-rimmed gray eyes.

He stands. His knees groan; one of them pops, but instead of pain, he feels a touch of sweet relief from the normal aches and pains of his aging body. He needs to get home before the storm comes, home to a quiet house, a lonely house.

In his mind, he hears the loud pop of a gun, and he's taken back to earlier that day . . .

Were you able to picture that? The setting, the older man, the birds, his heartache? Were you able to look into the man's sad, red-rimmed eyes? Do you have questions about the gun, the events of earlier in the day, or the man's obvious sadness? If so, I did my job as a writer. If not, well, maybe I didn't do my job so well after all.

Writing is a simple thing made difficult by most everyone who attempts to do it. There are rules and more rules and even more rules that someone came up with years ago (probably before most of us were born) that we adhere to, even if they are outdated and don't necessarily apply to today's world. One of those rules is not outdated, and it's a valuable tool for budding writers to learn.

Hook the reader early. Yup, that's it. Hook the reader early. Some will say you need to hook them in the first sentence, others say the first paragraph, while others say the first chapter (if it's a longer work). For me, I believe in hooking a reader as early as possible, whether it's the first sentence, first paragraph, first page, or first chapter. The earlier, the better.

The goal is to engage the reader early, then keep them engaged. Create a setting but without giving every little detail. Create a character (their physical appearance). Create mood using the setting, the weather, the character's temperament, thoughts, or actions. Create connection by making the setting and characters feel as believable and relatable as possible. Create questions for the reader.

In the 325 words above, I created a setting (a park), a character (an old man), an impending event (a storm), an emotion (that man's sadness), and, hopefully, some intrigue (the sound of a gun's pop). The goal was to set the story up in under a page—in this case, four paragraphs.

The hardest part of this, at least for me, is creating relatability.

Most writers can see the scene in their heads. I can't. What I see is a black space. As I tell the story, the black space gives way to the colors of the picture I paint. In this case, the man sitting on the bench was the only thing I saw. Then the park came into focus with the pigeons pecking at the ground, scooping up bread, and eating it, the red brick sidewalk with the weeds growing up between the spaces.

Unfortunately, that's window dressing without something relatable.

What can I do to make the reader relate to the story I am about to tell? Sadness. Everyone has been sad at some point in their life, which means the reader can relate to how the old man feels. I knew right away the man was older and very sad. Creating the man's sadness wasn't just about the red-rimmed eyes or the tears in them. It was also the impending storm. The gray and black clouds coincide with the gray world the man experiences emotionally.

To create that sadness, I showed the man's tears and how it mingled with the sweat on his face. I also mentioned he needs to get home before the storm comes, home to a quiet house, a lonely house. There's also the gunshot and how he hears it and it takes him back to earlier in the day. The implications of this one sentence hold so much weight to it because of another sentence a few lines before. In reference to putting lotion on his bald head to protect it, this sentence appears: *Lillian would have made sure he did that.*

Tears follow right after that sentence.

There's one more thing going on here. For most readers, it's subliminal; but for writers, it's intentional. Colors. Colors create mood and connection and are powerful descriptors. The man's clothes indicate a simple wardrobe full of browns and tans. His hair is white, so even if I don't mention he is older, you get the impression he is. The red brick path also feels like something old, while the green grass brings a little light to the story, as does the light blue sky above him. The birds are gray and white, and most people would guess they're pigeons because of both their colors and the fact the man is feeding them.

That first paragraph sets up what could be a light-hearted story. When you get to the second one, the colors become ominous. The gray and black clouds and his red-rimmed eyes completely change the outlook of the story. For me, the gray, black, and red combination greatly reflect the colors of sorrow.

All of these things are intended to create relatability, and if, as a writer, you are able to create that one trait, you have a great chance of hooking your readers beyond the first page or chapter.

It's always a great idea to hook the readers early. The sample given above is from a prequel to another story that has a killer first sentence, one I feel hooks the reader right off the bat:

He woke to the sound of a memory, one involving a gunshot.

Create relatability early in your story and you can hook your readers for the long haul. Give it a shot. It's one of the things I know so far.

Until we meet again, my friends, be kind to one another.

MAXWELL I. GOLD

I FEEL SO ALIVE

Wrapped within the blackest moments of our worst nightmares, a monster stirred, restless and cruel. The bastard of a nameless god, awoken from deathless slumber, prepared to lay waste to a helpless world. Voices so coarse and filled with wrath flooded the skylines where steel and concrete spires curdled like wiry toothpicks beneath the horrendous chords and marble foundations cracked and settled further towards the center of oblivion.

I saw the streets packed with flesh and fragile spirit, bodies unable to comport themselves, drunk on anxiety and dread. The existential wonderment beleaguered even the soundest minds while, above me, the purpled firmaments blended with a crimson dawn; too late to resist the crushing music of a grotesque and immense force willing to swallow everything. The screams were drowned out, forced to reconcile their own pitiful existence whereupon a heavy, toxic murk pressed over the last cities, oceans, and fortress-anthills of sapient resistance. One by one, I watched the fire, smoke, and death mushroom towards a star-riddled graveyard, my laughter billowed endlessly into the bosom-bones of night, and I'd never felt so alive standing on the corpse of the Earth.

Dark Fashion with Diana Olney

Part One
Demons on Display: The Electrifying Vision of Alexander McQueen

Jack the Ripper Stalks His Victims. Highland Rape. Nihilism. Banshee. Whether emblazoned on a fluorescent marquee or a technicolor billboard or a grayscale headline in the paper, you wouldn't readily associate the bold, bleeding ink of titles like these with the glamorous world of high fashion. Such audacious themes, with their grim imagery and violent histories, were never in vogue, never in style, never trendy anywhere but a dark theater or the cracked spine of a horror novel.

Until Alexander McQueen came along.

Today, Alexander McQueen is an iconic name in fashion, but in his prime, McQueen was more than a designer. He was an artist, a storyteller, fluent in the language of nightmares. Bumps in the night. Screams from a screen. Crimson stains on satin. These elements were as essential to McQueen's work as needle and thread, brazen stitches in a tapestry that blurred the line between beauty and terror. "I find beauty in the grotesque," McQueen once said, a skill he avidly put to use for nearly two decades. Over the course of his career, McQueen did for fashion what horror movies had been doing for the screen for decades: he subverted expectations, bending the straight and narrow path of the runway into daring new shapes and uncharted constellations.

You don't need to be fashion forward to appreciate the striking innovation of McQueen's methods. For the first several years of his career, Lee Alexander McQueen— "Lee" to friends and family—was a long way from luxury himself. From his time studying design at St Martins in London to the curation of his debut collections, McQueen and his modest team didn't have the means to cover dinner, let alone the steep cost of couture. Living on unemployment, what little funds he received were used to sustain his fledgling brand, a fashion house built from a foundation of resourceful ingenuity. Like an avant-garde fairy tale, McQueen forged garments from the very fabric of the world around him, turning the mundane into runway gold. A black trash bag became a sheath dress. Plastic wrap layered like gauze was bound skintight around a model. A blazer patterned with haphazard tire marks was thrust into the spotlight, then later tailored as wardrobe for rock icon David Bowie. McQueen didn't just think outside the box, he thrived there, a talent that set his eccentric, uninhibited aesthetic apart from the polished tableau in the pages of *Vogue*.

In regard to his fashion shows, McQueen said, "You should walk out either repulsed or exhilarated, or I'm not doing my job." But what he didn't say, at least not in the early days of his career, was where his penchant for shock and awe came from. McQueen was viewed as a rebel, a tempest storming the fashion capitals like a bull in a posh china shop, but behind the scenes, he was wrestling his own monsters. A sufferer of depression and victim of childhood abuse, his life's darkness had deep, twisted roots. But he didn't hide from it. Like so many artists throughout history, McQueen's inner demons were his greatest muse, and he didn't just face them—he set them loose, strapping his devils into nosebleed stilettos and sending them straight onto the runway.

From there, McQueen's vision bloomed, spawning dark reveries like resurrected heads on a bloodthirsty hydra. The resulting

menagerie was untamable, a designer chimera that was more feral than fashionable. One season, models sprouted towering horns and antlers; the next, predatory eyes and jagged claws. But this wild energy wasn't limited to visuals. In the grip of McQueen's high-octane fashions, the pageantry of haute couture became a theatrical performance, setting a dramatic tone for the garments with ominous music and elaborate backdrops that on several occasions literally went up in flames. During the debut of his 1997 collection, *It's a Jungle Out There*, an accidental fire broke out, an incident that gained notoriety when McQueen refused to put out the blaze until the show was over. A year later, in his Autumn collection, *Joan*, McQueen reimagined the death of the famous French martyr by staging a ring of fire around a masked model—right in the middle of the catwalk. Much like his creations, McQueen was unabashedly fearless, a fact made increasingly apparent as the budget of his brand grew. Additional highlights include the starkly infernal *Dante*, an eerie procession of skeletal accessories on a crucifix-shaped runway in a church designed by an alleged Satanist; and *Voss*, an ode to Victorian mental asylums shown from the voyeuristic view of a two-way mirror. Ensconced by white padded walls, the collection was a madhouse of bandaged, straightjacketed models and featured a grand finale of a nude woman in an enclosure filled with live moths, all set to the harrowing soundtrack of a throbbing, Poe-esque heartbeat.

In an additional dose of dread, McQueen also created several collections as direct homage to classic horror films. Juxtaposed by frozen scenery, 1999's *The Overlook* paid tribute to Stanley Kubrick's *The Shining* with dense overcoats and ghost-white makeup. In a similarly chilling vein, *The Birds* (1995) boasted startling, anxious designs inspired by the infamous Hitchcock film as well as the ophthalmic works of artist M.C. Escher; while *Supercalifragilisticexpialidocious* (2002) took macabre notes from the films of Tim Burton, particularly the late nineties bloody favorite, *Sleepy Hollow*.

But McQueen's influences weren't just in the past. His work was also a reflection of the present, a hall of mirrors framing the real-life horrors he saw around him. In *The Horn of Plenty*, McQueen produced a scathing commentary on the excess of high fashion, accosting audiences with a massive junkyard heap centerpiece surrounded by swarms of black-clad women who looked more like spectres than models. This raw, haunted ambiance was a staple of the times as the "heroin chic" trend swept the nation, climbing everything from billboard charts to the raw-boned statures of supermodels. Fashion had taken a dark turn—a turn that paralleled McQueen's meteoric ascendancy.

There were bumps in the road, of course. Success came quickly to McQueen, though not so quickly as to spare him criticism. By age twenty-seven, he was made creative director of revered fashion label Givenchy, a highly coveted position; but even as he rose to the top, balancing both his role at Givenchy and the growth of his own brand, McQueen's provocative ideas weren't always met with praise. His inaugural collections, particularly those that featured battered women, were met with judgment that was just as aggressive as the exhibitions. When battalions of models ruffled fashion week feathers with slashed-up ensembles and dangerously low waistlines, the press spurned McQueen, calling his work vulgar and misogynistic.

Despite the controversy, McQueen never apologized. He said he wanted "to make women look stronger" and he couldn't accomplish that by allowing them to seem "innocent and naïve." The loss of his own innocence was on blatant display, but the art of facing demons was a two-way street.

Though McQueen's dark corpus was not without glimmers of light. In his final collection, *Plato's Atlantis*, he brought the opulence of both the modern and natural world to the runway, creating dazzling images of rebirth with prismatic digital printing and ethereal makeup. After McQueen's tragic suicide in 2010, this lighter tone lived on in the posthumous continuation of his legacy. Under the leadership of new creative director Sarah Burton, who began as an intern for the fashion house, McQueen's aesthetic was finessed with a woman's touch while preserving the bold beating heart of his work. The ensuing collections were a renaissance of Victorian elegance, crafting gothic fantasies silhouetted, beaded, and corseted in a timeless hourglass of romanticism.

Nearly fifteen years later, the blazing shadow McQueen left behind still hasn't faded. In 2021, the house of McQueen paid tribute to its fearless namesake with the perfect statement piece: a dress so violently bloodied it would raise alarm if worn on the street. Conversely, the brand's most iconic symbol, the playfully morbid skull motif, is more prevalent than ever. Even if you can't afford the steep price tag on the printed scarves and bedazzled jewelry, you've likely seen the knockoffs: hordes of grinning black skulls in acrylic and cotton scattered like miniature Memento Mori's along the walls of department stores, a catacomb of consumerism that McQueen would surely satirize if he were here today.

But Lee Alexander McQueen gave us more than just commentary. He saw the world through a kaleidoscopic lens, a gift that enabled him to reimagine his craft again and again. That was his true passion—not to simply shape fabric for a garment but to *remake* it into a new medium. A medium that went beyond style, beyond beauty, beyond the finite armor layered between flesh and the elements. From the first stitch in a seam to the final pair of sky-high heels to exit the runway, McQueen's work was always evolving, an experience that transcended fashion's narrow measurements.

PHOTO CREDIT TO EDWARD DOSE   EDWARDDOSEPHOTOGRAPHY.COM

THE DAY I QUIT WRITING

BY JOHN R. LITTLE

I wrote my first short story when I was 12 years old. It was not memorable.

I *sold* my first story when I was 26. For those intervening 14 years, I wrote more than 200 stories, and I learned my craft from every one of them.

I sold my first novel 25 years later. It was published when I was 51. Since then, I've written and published 25 books.

I've won the Bram Stoker Award and the Black Quill Award, along with being nominated for both of them many other times.

All in all, when I look back at my career, I have nothing to complain about. I'm very fortunate to have found a loyal fan base, and most reviewers have been very kind to me.

All that changed on June 8, 2023.

\#

My daughter, Peri, was born on December 23, 1975. She was named Persephone after the 10th planet in our solar system, according to a Larry Niven novel (perhaps it was *Protector*, but I can't remember with certainty).

Persephone was the Greek Goddess companion to Pluto, God of the Underworld. She brought us spring every year. It was a pretty cool name but a bit of a mouthful, so we gave her the nickname Peri.

When she was growing up, Peri and I used to do science experiments together. She loved science and so did I.

Every Christmas, regardless of other presents, I always gave her the year-end issue of *Discover* magazine that outlined the year's most interesting and important science breakthroughs. We would compare notes after we'd both read the issue.

When Peri got married, she wanted a medieval themed wedding, outdoors, celebrating life and love. I was dressed like a 14th century king, and she was a beautiful princess. It was a wonderful time when I walked her down the garden aisle, sun shining, birds chirping.

Much later, on June 7 of last year (2023), Peri was in the hospital with bacterial meningitis. She was 47 years old. The meningitis alone would have been severe enough, but the next morning, an aneurism in her brain blew, putting her in a deep coma. Shortly after that, she had a massive stroke, which was the final straw.

Three horrible incidents within 24 hours, each of which alone could have killed her. She didn't stand a chance.

My daughter was declared brain dead, and the following day, she was disconnected from the machines keeping her alive. It was the right call (by her husband) since there was not a chance in hell she would ever recover.

Although I didn't realize it immediately, that was the day I gave up writing.

\#

Her death rocked me in ways I wouldn't have ever anticipated. The most obvious thing was that I was very depressed. I loved Peri, but we'd been having a big disagreement for some time. I felt horribly guilty about that. So, I was filled with a combination of despair and guilt.

I was more irritable than I'd ever been.

I felt afraid whenever I was separated from my wife. It turns out humans have a psychological attachment system built in with our loved ones, and when one gets ripped out (like Peri did), the brain worries about losing the others, even when there's no reason. Unreasonable panic can result.

I couldn't sleep well. I had trouble focusing.

Old traumas from my childhood suddenly reared their ugly heads.

It was like all my plans, feelings, emotions, and memories were all shaken apart, tossed in the air, and fell back down in a chaotic mess.

I feared death for myself much more than I usually do.

My wife, smartie that she is, suggested I go to a psychologist, which I did. I ended up having weekly sessions for about 8 months.

I had no urge to write.

Soon after, I realized it was worse than that. I actively hated everything I'd ever written before. I'd stare at the copies of my books and the magazines with my stories in them, and all I wanted to do was throw them in the garbage. That's what they deserved.

And I sure as hell didn't want to ever write anything else. That would be crazy, to try to create even more of that crap.

Over the next few months, there were many times I really was close to just dumping everything. The posters on our walls of my book covers? Belonged in the dump. Manuscripts stored on my computer? Needed to be zapped into oblivion. And of course, the books themselves? They should be shredded.

I kept this all to myself. I didn't mention it to my wife or my psychologist. I just tried to shove the feelings away, not wanting to think about them.

One thing kept nagging at me, though. I'd long promised myself that one day I would write a memoir, talking about my experiences with writing in the small press. I thought my fans would enjoy reading that. It had felt for years that I somehow owed it to them.

It was always a project for "someday."

But . . . what if someday never came? If Peri could die so young, there was certainly no guarantee that I would live long enough for "someday" to arrive.

I had to write just one more book. I needed to get this behind me, even if it was going to be just another pile of crap. I was living with enough guilt about Peri; I didn't want to add to it by not doing what I'd long promised myself.

So, about two months after her death, I started my research. I found boxes full of notes made 40 and 50 years ago, notes my younger self wrote, pieces of stories, completed manuscripts, letters, and, eventually, contracts and published works.

I read through these old artifacts, and I remembered how my younger self was so excited about everything. I relived the joy when he wrote his very first short story. He knew without any doubt whatsoever that he was going to be a writer one day, and he pounded stories out day after day. He cheered when he got rejection letters from editors if they suggested ways to improve his stories. He shrugged from form rejection letters, just sending the rejected story out to a different magazine.

He was overjoyed just at having the opportunity to write.

I re-read all these memories, and I organized my memoir. I wrote it over the next six months or so, and I tried to bring the excitement that I knew young John would have been feeling. The old, frail letters and notes were like opening a treasure box full of surprises.

As I was writing the book, I was seeing my psychologist every week. Lina (not her real name) helped me get past Peri's death and all the associated messes my mind had ripped to pieces.

As I was healing in Lina's sessions, I was taking a parallel journey back through my writing career, and that trip back in time was healing my writing soul. I hadn't actually realized that while doing the writing. I felt like I was just meeting my obligation.

By the end of 2023, most of my memoir was complete, and I realized a surprising thing: most of my writing brain was back the way it should have been. I no longer hated my books and stories. I'd lived through their creation, publication, and reader response in such detail, it was like living that part of my life completely over again.

Writing the memoir started as an obligation. It ended up as a path to finding my love of writing once again. I'm as excited about my

future projects as my teenaged self was about sending off a new story to *Galaxy* or *Amazing Stories*.

I had expected *My Quirky Little Memoir* to be my last book. Now, it looks like there's going to be many more to follow.

I hope my fans follow me to whatever destination I embark upon.

John R. Little is an award-winning author of suspense, dark fantasy, and horror.

He currently lives in Ayr, a small town near Kitchener, Canada, and is always at work on his next book. John has published 25 books to date, and most of them are available here. He hopes you enjoy his work.

Find More of John's Books On

THE PARANORMAL PASTOR

Bizarre Oddities of a Haunted Soul

By Ezekiel Kincaid

The daily grind of life has a way of eroding every ounce of wonder in our souls. When we were young and free from the burdens and responsibilities of life, our minds had the liberty to ponder the mysteries, oddities, and unexplained phenomena in our world. As we enter adulthood, something happens. Especially when times of trial and uncertainty hit. We find ourselves in survival mode. Our minds focus on jobs, raising children, building a career, financial crises, and looming health issues. All these things monopolize our mental and emotional energy, leaving us little time to step back and recapture the things that once made life so grand.

One of the reasons I started writing horror was to try and preserve my childhood wonder of the unexplained and weird. I can still recall the feelings I had when I was six years old, watching *The Demon Murder Case* and *The Midnight Hour* for the first time. My pursuit of horror, comics, and writing has been to preserve these moments and pass them down to my readers. I want to help keep that dying ember alive in your soul and fan it into flames.

But there's another tension in life when it comes to the known and the unknown. It's objective scientific reality versus subjective personal experience. There is often a dichotomy present (on both sides, unfortunately) that evolutionary science has done away with the need for anything paranormal and supernatural. This is unfortunate, since the goal of science is just to explain the laws and processes in the world. As a man of science and faith, I feel this tension and walk the tightrope with extreme caution. I'm a huge proponent of the compatibility between religion (mainly Christianity because it is my faith tradition) and science. I've written, taught, and spoken on these subjects many times over the course of my life.

This tension has led me into the field of paranormal investigation. Many people look at my life from the outside and scratch their heads. "Wait a minute, Zeke. You're a pastor, have three theology degrees, hold to evolutionary science, write horror, and are a paranormal investigator? Dude, how does that even work?" How this all fits together is another topic for another time. What is important is the tension I am talking about that keeps me balanced.

To be fair, I am one of the most skeptical paranormal investigators I know. There has been a lot I have seen and experienced that can be dismissed as overactive imaginations, old houses and electrical problems, manipulation, and just plain faking it. This grieves me and is unfortunate because it gives the field a bad name.

With all the "unexplained" phenomena I have been able to explain away, there are certain experiences still haunting me to this day. These are the ones I want to share with you in this article. When I'm done, I also want to leave something in your own hands to investigate.

As a skeptical paranormal investigator, there are two events I cannot explain. The first one happened on an investigation, and the second was a personal encounter.

While on an investigation at a famous historical house in Kentucky, I experienced my first run in with poltergeist phenomenon. When I go to a property, I am careful to guard myself against what I call "priming." Priming can be intentional or unintentional. It is when people who have been to said place start to tell you about everything they have experienced there. Then they get other people involved who have had similar encounters at the same place, and they begin to bombard you with their stories. This is where we have to be on guard with having our mental and emotional state "primed" to experience something that isn't really there.

I've been a paranormal investigator for almost as long as I have been in ministry. I've learned how to guard my mind and take in the information and testimonies without being swayed by them. When I investigate a place, I am open, yet at the same time, I am itching to prove it wrong. Some could say I am biased towards skepticism, and there might be an element of truth to that; I don't know. What I do know is this approach has kept me from attributing things to the paranormal and supernatural that shouldn't be. But it has also helped me be open to those things which defy reason.

Back to the poltergeist. My team and I were the only people in the house. I am fortunate to have an awesome team that doesn't fake stuff or read into every odd thing as a paranormal event. This is especially true with my friend, investigator, and founder of our team, Dustin. While exploring this home, he and I witnessed the mannequins in the house move and facial expressions change.

At first, I didn't believe what I saw. That was until I was standing face to face with the mannequin, along with a picture of its face we had taken earlier, and saw it had changed. It wasn't something huge like going from a smile to a frown. It was in the corner of the lips and their length. It was around the eyes and how they were opened. It was seeing the hand of the mannequin move a few centimeters. It was enough to make this skeptic pause and wonder what in the world was going on in this home.

The activity didn't end there. Later on in the night, while Dustin and I were sitting on the front porch, we watched one of our headlamps take flight. The light was sitting in a chair, untouched. We both heard the scraping sound of the plastic light being dragged across the wooden chair. When we looked over, we saw the light fly off the chair and across the porch, where it landed close to the steps.

To this day, I have found no natural explanation for these experiences.

Many of my fans and readers will be familiar with the second phenomenon I'm about to share. I have spoken of it on podcasts, talked about it in interviews, and written about it in the forward of my book *The Dawning*. It's the story of the little girl, Theodosia. Before I saw her ghost, I was a healthy skeptic when it came to stories about full body apparitions.

The first time I encountered Theo was in a dream. I had been writing what is now called my Dreadful Death series. It was supposed to be a horror fantasy about a little girl named Theodosia Whitfield who could live in both the supernatural and natural world simultaneously.

The night she appeared, we were standing in her farmhouse. She had lost her look of innocence. Her face was twisted with a sinister grin, and the skin was peeling off. She told me, "The way you wrote my story is all wrong. I want to show you how it really happened." In the dream, she proceeded to take me around the house and property. What she showed me was so horrific, it changed the entire direction and storyline of the book series.

This wasn't the unexplainable part. That came a few days later when I sat down to make the changes. Theodosia appeared in my room as a full body apparition. This happened on and off for a period of almost three years until I finished the books. She would appear, tell me what she wanted in the story, then leave. My last encounter with her was back in June of 2021, four months before the series got picked up for publication. I haven't seen or heard from her since. There is much more that happened with her during this time period, but it is beyond the scope of this article.

These two encounters are what keep me searching, investigating, and writing. The mystery and fascination are alive and well within my soul, in spite of the harsh skepticism I carry around in my back pocket.

I said I wanted to leave you with something to investigate on your own, so here it is: The advances in quantum physics have opened up an entirely new world for all of us. What if I told you there is a sound theory, backed by sound scientists, that is making progress on the existence of consciousness after death being a real thing?

That's what is happening with the Orch OR theory. Orchestrated Objective Reduction (Orch Or) was founded by Roger Penrose and Stuart Hameroff. It basically says consciousness is a result of quantum fluctuations in the brain. This oscillation of quantum fluctuation and processing is able to continue after death, thus giving rise to the idea that consciousness can continue to exist after the body has shut down.

So, my dear readers, is this life all there is, or is there something beyond our own sight, sounds, and taste? My research and experiences inform me there is more than we could ever dare to think or imagine. Guard your fascination and wonder of life with jealousy. If you don't, the daily grind will snuff it out, and that bright spark in your soul will soon follow. Until next time, enjoy the mystery and revel in the unknown.

Zeke

Have you ever wanted to read a book from the point of view of a serial killer? Have you ever rooted for the bad guy to win? This book will make you cry, cheer and cringe at the gruesomeness it holds. Come with me as we delve into the origin story of the most infamous ghost from Nightmare Island, and watch as he slowly descends into madness.

HORROR ANTHOLOGY CALL

SKG AUTHOR SERVICES IS LAUNCHING OUR FIRST HALLOWEEN ANTHOLOGY IN 2025.

THE THEME IS –
WHAT LURKS IN THE DARKNESS?

WE ARE OPEN FOR SUBMISSIONS.

GENRE: HORROR – EXTREME WILL BE CONSIDERED, BUT NO SA, ANIMAL CRUELTY, EROTICA OR HARM TO CHILDREN. TRIGGER WARNINGS SHOULD BE INCLUDED.
WORD COUNT – UP TO 10K.
PAYMENT – ROYALTY SPLIT
SUBMISSIONS DUE – AUG 1ST, 2025.
PUBLICATION DATE –SEPT 15TH 2025

SEND TO SKGAUTHORSERVICES@GMAIL.COM
ACCEPTANCE EMAIL WILL BE SENT WITHIN 2 WEEKS OF SUBMISSION DATE.
SUBMISSIONS MUST BE PROFESSIONALLY EDITED.

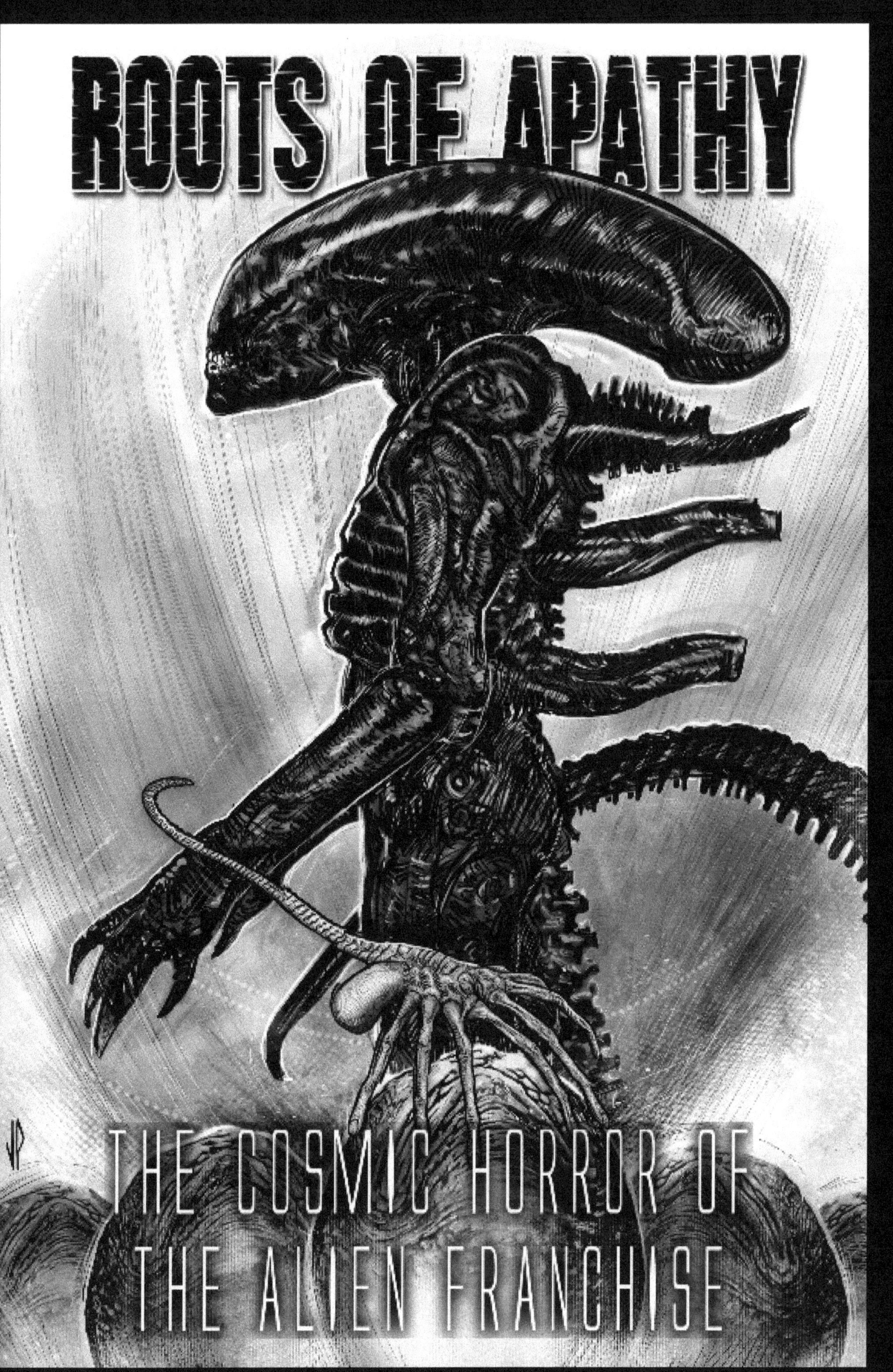

ROOTS OF APATHY
THE COSMIC HORROR OF
THE ALIEN FRANCHISE

ROOTS OF APATHY: HOW THE ALIEN FRANCHISE GAVE THE MASSES COSMIC HORROR

BY THOMAS R CLARK

Note: For those of you new to this column, I started ROOTS OF APATHY in the first issue of the former HOUSE OF STITCHED magazine. Feel free to discover these on Amazon! Its purpose is to educate readers on the history of cosmic horror, particularly through the most popular pieces inspired by Lovecraft's Cthulhu world. The first four columns focused on H.P. Lovecraft's circle of friends and the mutual Cthulhu sandbox they played in. Those friends included the solitary Robert E. Howard and mad poet/artist Clark Ashton Smith, as well as publisher August Derleth and Lovecraft's pupil, the legendary Robert Bloch. The content has since shifted to the films inspired by this brand. We've already touched on the Predators (in STRANGER WITH FRICTION ISSUE #9, also available on Amazon), so now it's time to explore their eternal enemies . . .

"IN SPACE, NO ONE CAN HEAR YOU SCREAM."

This tag line started it all, one could say. It's simple, direct, and to the point. Between the title and this sentence, you knew what you were in for going into a screening of Ridley Scott's *ALIEN*. A film the studio initially didn't have faith in, dismissing it as a disposable B-movie sci-fi jaunt, it both terrified and enthralled audiences. Shot on a budget of $11 million, *ALIEN* went on to inspire a half-billion-dollar franchise and crossed over with the subject of the last edition of this column ("PREDATORS & PREY, THE COSMIC HORROR OF THE PREDATOR FRANCHISE"). But why was it successful not only in popularity but in essentially reintroducing Mr. and Mrs. John Q. Public to cosmic horror?

On the surface, *ALIEN* is part of a renaissance in science fiction. This movement started in the wake of *2001: A Space Odyssey* and was in response to that film's clean room aesthetic. The "lived-in" quarters of outer space gave us a perception not seen in science fiction before. It allowed the blue-collar workers of Middle America to see science fiction from their point of view and opened the doors to telling new stories. John Carpenter's *Dark Star*, Douglas Trumbull's *Silent Running*, and Disney's *The Black Hole*—a film we will discuss in a future column, alongside *Event Horizon*—which came out later in the same year, all shared the aesthetic. *Outland*, also written by *ALIEN* screenwriter Dan O'Bannon, further enforced this window dressing. Due to its similarities in sets and props, many fans see Peter Hyam's 1981 reimagining of *High Noon* as being attached to the *ALIEN* world.

I talked to *ALIEN* fan Kristin Dearborn, author of *The Amazing Alligator Girl* and *Faith of Dawn*, about this and why the film works so well. Much of it is a result of Dan O'Bannon's script, filled with all the fears of an adolescent, from having an omniscient "Mother" dictating our daily chores to the sexual metaphors present in the infamous chest-burster scene. But what was it about O'Bannon's screenplay that made this film work so well? I've already touched on its aesthetic appeal and subtle themes. Ms. Dearborn agrees with me, but there's much more to it, she told me.

"Setting, antagonist, and character," she said. And she's right on target. *"O'Bannon transforms outer space into a banal, blue-collar environment."* It's not just O'Bannon who gets it done, it's Ridley Scott and his trademark pacing. *"Yes, those panning shots show us how vast it is, the Nostromo itself is a terrifying house of horrors, even without the xenomorph (though it's not called that until 1986's ALIENS, for simplicity's sake, I'm using the name now). Seriously, why does the Nostromo need the room where Brett meets his end with all those dangling chains and water dripping from the ceiling? Why does it need a sparkle light mother womb room to talk to the computer? BUT for those seven space truckers, the Nostromo is a job site. The movie opens with talk about shares.*

"So we have this banal yet terrifying space, these people who are just trying to do their jobs, who want to 'get home and party.' And their space is infected by . . . something. Science Officer Ash says to the surviving crew, 'You still don't understand what you're dealing with, do you? The perfect organism. Its structural perfection is matched only by its hostility . . . I admire its purity. A survivor, unclouded by conscience, remorse, or delusions of morality.' That description of the monster that O'Bannon conceived and H. R. Giger imagined and Ridley Scott directed and Bolaji Badejo brought to life is flawless. That killing machine, encountered on the 'almost primordial' LV-426, is a gooey, drippy, sexy nightmare, and it's lived rent free in our collective conscience since 1979. It manages to be insectile and humanoid at the same time; it looks simultaneously biological and mechanical. People give Lambert shit because she freaked out in the movie . . . I think she's the only one with a sensible response.

"Aside from the setting and the monster, the final piece that makes ALIEN so perfect can't, I don't think, be credited to O'Bannon. Ripley's part was originally written for a man but given to Sigourney Weaver with very few tweaks (I suspect if a male actor played the role, his underwear in the final scene may have been different, but we'll never know). Too often, writers try and write STRONG FEMALE CHARACTERS, in the process forgetting that women are people. Ripley is a person before she is a STRONG FEMALE CHARACTER (in ALIEN, anyway—I think her characterization is one of the few missteps in ALIENS, which is course corrected for in ALIEN3)."

And this is why I asked Kristin for her thoughts. I first saw *ALIENS* on its opening night, with a platoon of Marines sitting in the row before me. I've had the privilege of seeing these films through my lens. But to truly understand the impact of this franchise, and the character of Ripley in particular, I felt it best to seek the opinion of a person who would have bonded with the lead character for her representation on screen.

Outside of its appearance and the glass ceiling it broke in conjunction with *ALIENS* for female leads in action-oriented films, the *ALIEN* franchise is known as one of the best science-fiction horror franchises of all time. Yet, much like the Predator films, *ALIEN* and its descendants are more than simply science-fiction. They are pure cosmic horror, with an inspirational pedigree going back to Lovecraft himself. *ALIEN* is brilliant with this trope, not revealing the monster to viewers clearly until the third act. The film showed its innovation at recreating a subgenre of horror for a new generation. Gone were the tentacles and fish men. Instead, we are treated to bio-organic monsters using other beings as birthing creches.

"The idea of ALIEN," Kristin said, *"stripped down to its most base form, is very Lovecraft: we are not alone in the universe, and the other guys are AWFUL and completely indifferent to us . . . unless they can use us to incubate their young. We're not special; we're just there at the wrong place at the wrong time. The crew of the Nostromo is absolutely alone when they take on the xenomorph out there in hostile space. Even the ship itself feels vast and uncaring.*

"Where it may differ is the xenomorph as an animal. It's not an elder god; it's organic life with a life cycle, and the goals of any organic life: feeding and reproducing. The xenomorph in ALIEN isn't cruel or teasing; Jonesy the cat probably plays with his food more."

As we've discussed before, an AI search on Google will tell us cosmic horror consists of the following: The unknown or alien, forbidden knowledge, an overall conspiracy of some sorts, beings or entities that care nothing about humanity, insanity/madness surrounding phenomena that cannot be explained, all while contemplating the human experience and the humanness of the struggle. But I asked Ms. Dearborn, "What is cosmic horror to you?"

"Cosmic horror is the fear of the unknown," Dearborn told me. *"The bleakness that comes when we realize that humans aren't the be all, end all, that the world does not in fact revolve around us. When we realize God didn't put us here, there is no plan, and we are as significant as a cat, a cow, or a bug. We don't know what's out there; it could even be absolutely nothing, and that's pretty scary too. But Cosmic horror isn't fun if there's nothing out there . . . the unfathomable, indescribable horrors of the universe await."*

And this is what truly makes the *ALIEN* films cosmic horror as opposed to plain old *Lost in Space* sci-fi. I'll present Jordan Peele's *NOPE* or Lee Whannell's *Upgrade* as examples of the latter. Ms. Dearborn further elaborates on this. *"There's an element of cosmic horror too that touches on the idea of Icarus, of forbidden knowledge and flying too close to the sun,"* she said. *"When we actively go searching for forbidden knowledge, we tend to not like what's there when we find it. Science brings horrors, a la Frankenstein's monster, the Brundlefly, the Island of Dr. Moreau, or poor Charlie McGee. That's just imaginary science gone wrong. We also have millions of real-life victims, from what the Nazis did in the name of science to MK Ultra, radiation experiments, syphilis experiments . . . the list goes on and on. It all tracks back to the unknown—which is why what we don't see is scarier than what we do see, nine times out of ten."*

Be it on the page, screen, or stage, cosmic horror (and horror in general) works best when mashed-up with something else. Science fiction is as open to this blending as any other genre. And the *ALIEN* films check off most all the cosmic horror criteria, from the fear of the unknown to secret cults and apathetic entities. But there's more. It's the characters that make this series work.

"Throughout the entire film, everyone acts within their character," she said. *"No one is making stupid decisions in order for the direction to position them for a kill like a chess piece. The crew of the Nostromo are tired, they want to get home, and their actions and reactions all reflect that. Everyone's motivations become clear. There's a point in the film where we may think:* He's a science officer! Why would he break quarantine protocol?! *But that is explained as the story unfurls.*

"ALIEN is a film made up of perfect moments. The scene when Brett is killed and we see the cat reacting rather than explicit carnage. Science Officer Ash, who Ripley distrusts, is a FUCKING ROBOT. Then when she uncovers special order 937, he tries to kill her in a weird porn corner (which ties in perfectly with the space truckers and doesn't seem at all out of place) by jamming a porn magazine down her throat. There's the iconic, flawless dinner scene where Kane's indigestion gets the best of him—the cast was kept in the dark about what would happen, and their reaction to that first blood spatter is real. ALIEN is perfect moment layered on top of perfect moment, interspersed with quiet rooms and a roaming camera, building the tension until it explodes out the airlock. I found myself really enjoying the way the camera dragged itself over the ship, building tension. If I want nonstop action, I'll go to ALIENS."

We can't talk about *ALIEN* without talking about the xenomorph itself. Stan Winston's creation, inspired by the work of artist H.R. Geiger, is perhaps one of the most iconic movie monsters of all time. And Dearborn agrees. *"The confluence of really strong monster design and two really good scripts and casts was like lightning in a bottle. I haven't even talked about the sexy parts of the xenomorph yet, and I think it's impossible to ignore how the horrible sexual aspects of the Giger's monster design contribute to its allure. Kane is a hale and hearty space trucker, exploring and adventurous, and next thing we know, his face is being raped through his helmet and he's got a parasite keeping him alive. Scott has said that the decision was made for the xenomorph to attack a male character because the attack would have been less shocking on a woman. With a woman, it could have been seen as titillating. The xenomorph attack is something of an inversion of childbirth; Kane is impregnated through the mouth and the 'baby' is born through his chest. Giger's design makes it impossible to look away from these* creatures. They move in slinky ways, they're slick black latex, they're literally dripping for most of the movie. They're engineered to trigger the sexy parts of our brains while simultaneously scaring the shit out of us."

One cannot talk about the ALIEN films without touching on the polarizing sequels in the franchise. Outside of James Cameron's *ALIENS*, much of the content to come out—with the exception of the prolific written adaptations and interpretations—has been met with fan scrutiny. Now, with that being said, there's no denying the fans of these entries, from *ALIEN3* to *ALIEN: Covenant*, exist.

"I've already used the word 'perfect' more than once to describe ALIEN," Ms. Dearborn adds. *"Cameron's ALIENS, I would argue, is an inferior film, but a hell of a lot more fun, and if I were asked to pick one of the two to watch on a random Saturday evening, I'd probably pick ALIENS. I don't think they could have gotten it so right a third time, or a fourth. ALIEN3 went through production hell before it was made. I'd love to see it as Fincher envisioned from the beginning—I bet that would be a killer film. I still like ALIEN3. I love the way Cameron's perfect nuclear family was violently obliterated as soon as possible. I love the idea of a prison station, no weapons. I love that we get to see what happens when the xenomorph uses another creature as a host. I love Ridley's noble sacrifice in the face of Bishop 2 (or Charles Weyland?). ALIEN: RESURRECTION gets a little harder to defend, but come on, there's Winona Ryder! There's that swimming xenomorph scene! Ron Perlman! Very early Joss Whedon! But alas, there's also that fucking newborn hybrid thing, but A3 and A:R took really wild and crazy risks with the IP that I don't think writers and directors could get away with today. And from there, it's all downhill. The AVP films were just so . . . basic. Boring. Uninteresting. What should have been the COOLEST MOVIE SHOWDOWN EVER was just lame. 'Whoever wins, we lose.' Know who lost? The audience.*

"A good xenomorph story needs more than the most iconic monster to grace the silver screen. We have to care about the people, and we need to stand behind their decision-making. In ALIEN and ALIENS, characters make proactive decisions that audiences can understand and relate to. These aren't slasher flicks, where the point is to see the cool kills. The characters and the stories have gotten weaker and weaker since ALIEN3, and it's hard to go from Ripley, Dallas, Ash, Hicks, Newt, Bishop to... I don't remember any character names beyond ALIENS, to be honest."

"Not all Alien stories play out on the big screen, however. In the last decade, Titan Books has put out some pretty baller novels by authors like Christopher Golden, Tim Lebbon, Tim Waggoner, Mira Grant, the late James A. Moore, and Weston Ochse. I especially enjoyed Mary SanGiovanni's ALIEN: ENEMY OF MY ENEMY and, most of all, V. Castro's ALIENS: VASQUEZ. There are the Dark Horse Comics, and the video games too. There's more out there than the movies for xenomorph fans!"

Which brings us to the ALIEN movie we have yet to see, *ALIEN: Romulus*. Originally planned as a television series for FX, it's since found a new lease with a forthcoming HULU release. The initial buzz of this being a series was at first met with some trepidation from franchise fans, but with Fede Alvarez (*Don't Breathe*) behind the helm, support seems to have risen. It's also set in that netherzone between *ALIEN* and *ALIENS*, and the network broadcasting the feature has a positive track record.

"Hulu brought us PREY, which I would argue is the best Predator film. The director is a competent horror director, so that's good. Neither the trailer nor the premise give us much of anything to go on, but I'm excited about where it falls in the timeline—between ALIEN and ALIENS with Ripley still in stasis. I will see it on opening weekend for sure, but I'm afraid to get my hopes up."

We'll all see what type of film Alvarez has made when *ALIEN: Romulus* hits streaming in August.

I'd like to thank Ms. Dearborn for her enthusiastic answers to my questions and encourage all of our readers to pick up one of her books. Next month, we are taking a trip to the Antarctic for a John Carpenter film some say is the perfect cosmic horror piece, and to ask, among other, um, *THINGS* . . . the question: "Who goes there?"

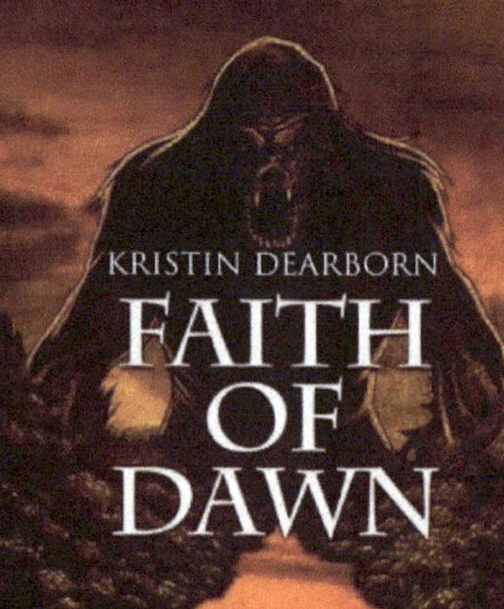
KRISTIN DEARBORN
FAITH OF DAWN

THE ORIGINS OF COSMIC HORROR
DON'T GO MAD!
A MEMENTO MORI INK EXCLUSIVE COLUMN
PUBLISHED TRI-ANNUALLY

THOMAS R CLARK
WHIRLWIND
THE CHIRPING IS
THE LAST THING
YOU'LL HEAR...

THOMAS R CLARK
ROOTS OF APATHY
FEATURING INTERVIEWS
WITH HORROR'S COSMIC
HORROR MASTERS!

This Summer...

Old School Creature Feature meets Halloween.

The Ojanox
Book I
Scream in the Dark

Daemon Manx

July 16

The Ojanox
Book II
Ashes to Ashes

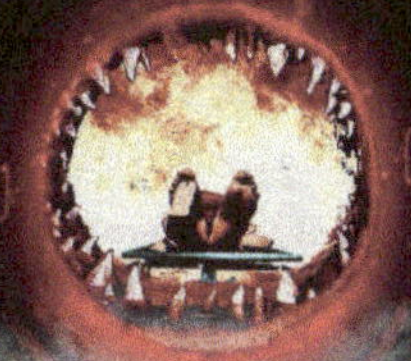

Daemon Manx

Aug 6

The Ojanox Series

The Ojanox
Book III
All Fall Down

Daemon Manx

Sept 3

The Ojanox
Book IV
Lonesome Mountain

Daemon Manx

Oct 1

By Daemon Manx
Available at
Barnes & Noble, Amazon, and www.lastwaltzpublishing.com

EVIL LITTLE FUCKS
(Limited to 100 Numbered Hardcover copies)

Evil comes in fun-sized packages. Behind the facade of sweetness and light, there lurks a darkness that defies comprehension as the veil of innocence is cruelly stripped away to reveal something far more sinister. Journey through the twisted minds of evil children, those who are born not of childish whimsy, but rather sprout from the seeds of nightmares.

Presenting Evil Little Fucks, a curated anthology of horror stories penned by leading authors in the genre. Traverse a universe where humanity's own offspring unleash a level of brutality that surpasses the capabilities of most adults. Just remember, you brought them into this world, and you just might have to take them out.

This edition will only be available directly through Sinister Smile Press.

Details at: www.sinistersmilepress.com/elf-limited

This edition will feature:
Laminate hardcover with dust jacket
7" x 10" trim size
Customized interior design
Built in ribbon bookmark
Limited page with number between 1 and 100
Signature page hand signed by all the authors

The Devil's Doorway by Steven Pajak

Kate Emerson returns to her childhood home in Chicago after her father's sudden stroke, only to awaken a malevolent force lurking within his unfinished painting. As the entity grows stronger, feeding off Kate's grief and despair, she must delve into the artwork's sinister history and confront the encroaching darkness that threatens to consume her.

With help from an old friend, James Nowak, and the enigmatic medium Tiqua Lovett, Kate navigates the blurred lines between reality and nightmare, desperate to seal the portal the demon has opened. In a harrowing battle against the relentless evil presence, Kate must confront her darkest fears to reclaim her life, her family, and her sanity.

"The Devil's Doorway" is a gripping supernatural thriller that explores the depths of grief, the power of family bonds, and the unyielding strength of the human spirit in the face of unimaginable horror. Will Kate emerge victorious, or will she be forever lost in the twisted realm beyond the painting's frame? Step through "The Devil's Doorway" and confront the nightmare that awaits in this chilling tale of love, loss, and the eternal struggle between light and darkness.

www.sinistersmilepress.com/books

August 3, 2024
Pre-order now!

MATT FORGIT

Matt Forgit is an author from New York and has now settled in Massachusetts. Forgit says he enjoys writing horror books with a comedic element. His recent release, FELICITOUS, is an homage to 1970s cult movies and 1980s slashers.

"I'm a big fan of the final girl trope," Forgit said in an interview with our CEO, Lisa Vasquez. "Especially strong, intelligent, and capable women."

We're right there with you, Matt!

When discussing the comedic element in his writing, I asked Matt if it was something he considered when he puts pen to paper.

"That's a great question," he responded. "…I want the horror to be taken seriously. Like the violence and the gore should be taken seriously. So, I always tread the line very carefully and think very hard about that. I don't want you laughing when someone dies. I want you to be afraid. I want you to care for them."

Referring to the context of the humor, Forgit explained how he likes to keep the comedic elements with characters who are kind of goofy.

"I try to keep it within the conversation, but I want you to feel terror when something bad is happening."

Grab your copy today of FELICITOUS wherever books are sold and find out about Annie, whose husband passed away and decides to buy herself a Ghost Town.

Is she all alone in Gull Valley?

Find out when Annie learns about a murderous and deranged cult known as The Felicitous who used to live there, whose enigmatic leader and devoted members mysteriously disappeared decades ago.

Now, Annie fears that The Felicitous have returned to Gull Valley. Is it all in her head? Have the cult's vengeful spirits been resurrected from beyond the grave? Or have The Felicitous reemerged to give Annie a blood-soaked welcome to the town they once called home?

Librorum Redita
Reviews by Lisa Lee

John R. Little has been writing professionally for more than 40 years. To celebrate his 25th book, he wanted to do something special . . . tell his loyal fans everything they didn't know about his writing career.

John R. Little's *My Quirky Little Memoir: Confessions of a Small Press Writer* is not an autobiography, though it does have some fun (and not so fun) facts and anecdotes about his life. It is (as he states within) a memoir about his writing journey, and it is a delightfully engrossing read. I read the first half of the book in one sitting because I was loathe to put it down.

Authors and aspiring authors will thoroughly enjoy Little's insight into his writing processes and experiences with magazines, publishers, cover artists, other authors, fans, and other industry contacts. Fans and soon-to-be fans will be thoroughly entertained by Little's style and journey and personal

anecdotes. If you haven't read his work before, this will make you want to.

This book was not what I expected. It's so much more. I was amazed, impressed, and moved by the amount and nature of deeply personal information John shared as well as how poignantly he presented it. I say John because feel I got to know him, if not thoroughly at least on a meaningful level, such is the impact of his story here. I was delighted to read the first story he ever wrote, as that gem is included within and alone makes it all worth the price of admission (and I thought it was cute).

But wait; there's more!

There are pictures! Also included within is cover art and illustrations from his books over the years, pictures of the author with others at events, family photos, and more. And as an added bonus, the pictures are in color. I found John's shoutouts to some of his favorite artists to be a classy touch.

Also classy, he gives credit to those who helped him along the way as he shares his journey. This book is not just one man's journey but also food for thought regarding community within the industry, determination, and believing in oneself despite adversity.

Entertaining, evocative, and insightful, this is an excellent reading experience. When I finished and closed the book, I said, "Wow," out loud to no one and everyone.

Available in paperback and Kindle at Amazon.

COLLECTOR'S ITEM
Draw You In: Volume 1
By Jasper Bark

Can you disappear so completely only one person remembers you existed?

That's what comics creator Linda Corrigan asks when her editor disappears without a trace. Drawn into an FBI investigation by Agent McPherson, Linda and comics historian Richard Ford unearth a chilling link to the forgotten comic artist R. L. Carver, whose work might just hold the key to a series of mysterious disappearances.

As they explore Carver's life, they uncover the secret history of horror comics, the misfits, madcaps, and macabre masters who forged an industry, frightened a generation, and felt the heat of the Federal Government. They also stumble on the shadow history of the United States on a road trip that veers into the nation's dark underbelly, where forbidden knowledge and forgotten lore await them.

Described as "Kavalier and Clay meets Clive Barker," *Draw You In, Volume 1 – Collector's Item* is the first in a mind-bending trilogy of novels. It contains stories within stories that explore horror in all its subgenres, from quiet to psychological horror, from hardcore to cosmic horror.

A vivid, suspenseful, and gruesome story flowing with mystery and genre-defying horrors, *Collector's Item* is volume 1 of Jasper Bark's Draw You In trilogy, a horror thriller series that is sure to deliver a dark and intense reading experience.

Bark's characters are multifaceted, as real people are, making them interesting and entertaining themselves. The female lead character, Linda, is particularly impressive and well-written, both strong and vulnerable, a mix of determination and flaws and passion for her art, and the mystery surrounding her is a compelling force in the story. By contrast, Richard Ford is a colorful character, a dark comedy relief in the midst of the intensity and terror of this complex tale.

But the story's always the thing, and Jasper Bark weaves a graphic and captivating tale, taking us into a dark and volatile facet of the horror comic world where the line between reality and the fantastical has begun to blur and the secrets of a legendary artist may hold the key to a dark mystery in addition to the disappearances. But there is much more to this chilling tale than that. The author's skillful foreshadowing and horrifying interludes engage the mind and add to the developing mystery and tension and building dread. The disturbing prologue alone is brutally impactful and lingers in the mind.

Bark's poignant social subtext speaking to the challenges women face in industry, the struggles of professional artists in general, and regard for the elderly adds depth and a touch of realism that enhances the story overall and the horrors in particular. And that touch of realism is critical because there is something unnatural and frighteningly unreal happening to people in this incredible horror thriller.

This is a shelf-worthy and highly recommended read.

But as I said, this is volume 1.

There's more.

Volume 2 is *Secret Origins*.

Are there any barriers between fiction and reality?

Linda begins to wonder as *Draw You In, Vol 2 – Secret Origins* continues this epic tale. Once again, she puts her comic career on hold to join Richard and Agent McPherson in the hunt for R. L. Carver's lost graphic novel—*Tales That Draw You In*. Rumored to be cursed, this legendary work put every publisher who tried to print it out of business. But *Tales That Draw You In* might unlock more than just their case. It could be the key to the secret history of the United States.

I found *Secret Origins* to be an absolutely compelling read. Here, Jasper Bark takes you on a deep dive into the mysteries surrounding R. L. Carver and, as the title suggests, the origins of the dark and enigmatic occurrences and people from *Collector's Item*.

Draw You In Volume 3 is *Behind the Mask*.

Is the whole of history a convenient lie?

That's how it's beginning to look to Linda, Richard, and Agent McPherson as they hunt for *Tales That Draw You In*, cartoonist R. L. Carver's legendary lost work. The key to finding it could lie in a memory Linda's repressed, from when she was a captive of the serial killer Henry McLaughlin.

The sinister cabal known as the Shadows in the Cave is also keen to retrieve Linda's memory. Linda, Richard, and McPherson learn that more than their own lives hang in the balance.

Draw You In Volume 3 – Behind The Mask is the explosive finale to this mind-bending trilogy.

(Synopsis blurb shortened to avoid spoilers.)

As of the writing of this review, I have not yet partaken of Volume 3, but I am eagerly looking forward to it.

Available from Crystal Lake Publishing and on Amazon.com

ABOUT THE AUTHOR: JASPER BARK

www.jasperbark.com

Jasper Bark comes with a government health warning. Do not read his work unless you want your nerves shredded, your heart pounding, and your reality permanently warped. Just one of his stories can leave you addicted for life. Don't be fooled by the awards or the five stars reviews. These were left by sick and depraved people whose minds were twisted by his writing. Once upon a time they wore ties, said their prayers, and played sudoku, then they encountered his books. Now look at them. Do you really want to be one of those people?

THE HORROR AT PLEASANT BROOK

By Kevin Lucia

Crystal Lake Publishing

A Relentlessly Dark and Driving

Halloween Horror Tale

This Halloween, a malevolent, creeping horror invades a small, isolated town nestled deep in the Adirondacks. It cares nothing for this town's secrets, prejudices, or flaws. Its only desires are to consume everything in its path and spread until nothing else remains.

It is ancient, pitiless, and unstoppable.

It is the horror at Pleasant Brook.

Standing resolutely in its shadow is an unlikely alliance—the remnants, the forgotten, the outcasts, and the underestimated. As the malevolence swells, they emerge as the town's last bastion of defense, its only hope against an ancient, remorseless force that brooks no resistance when the town of Pleasant Brook becomes the battleground for a confrontation between humanity's resilience and an evil beyond imagination.

The Horror at Pleasant Brook by Kevin Lucia is relentlessly dark and driving. It's a phenomenal story, and I found myself thoroughly engrossed in it.

Lucia's character diversity is impressive, and the characters themselves are vivid and believable, complete with unfortunate flaws. They quickly come to life, becoming real people you feel for, feel with, like or dislike or want to smack upside the head. This evocative characterization is one factor in making the story so immersive.

Another factor is Kevin Lucia's storytelling. I really enjoy his writing style; it is itself immersive. His classic and classical stylistic use of parenthetical elements to create depth with brevity deserves a round of applause. As a reader, I enjoy the poignance. As an editor, I find it brilliantly done.

And, of course, the other factor in *The Horror at Pleasant Brook* being immersive is it's an incredible story. A rising evil at Halloween is a classic theme (one I personally love), but Kevin's take on it is uniquely his, as is his telling of it. The suspense and tension and unpredictable twists will keep you reading in spite of whatever else life demands—then keep you up at night pondering the brazen tale, the subtleties, the characters even, and whether or not a night light is in order.

That being said, readers with sensitivities should take note this novel contains extreme subject matter and content and has vivid description of the same. Although some compare this story to those of King, this is a much more intense read (in a good way, in my opinion).

The Horror at Pleasant Brook is a gripping, gut-twisting, relentlessly dark story told with masterful skill. It's a fantastic Halloween read and a highly recommended and shelf-worthy book in general. I loved it.

Available in Kindle, hardcover, and paperback on Amazon, and in hardcover and paperback at Barnes & Noble.

About the Author: Kevin Lucia

Kevin Lucia's short fiction has been published in many venues, most notably with Neil Gaiman, Clive Barker, David Morell, Peter Straub, Bentley Little, and Robert McCammon. His first novel, *The Horror at Pleasant Brook*, was released by Crystal Lake Publishing, October 2023.

WHAT WAITS IN THE SHADOWS
By Wil Forbis

How long can horrifying secrets stay buried?

Twenty years after watching her father's brutal murder, Lisa Kallman is on the verge of a dream life. Her father's killer is in prison, she has a job helping children who've suffered like her and she's about to be married.

But Lisa can't escape a foreboding dread that tells her danger is around the corner. And when she begins hearing strange voices and people around her vanish, she wonders if her own memories can be trusted.

Is Lisa going mad, or is something evil and inhuman stalking her?

What Waits in the Shadows by Wil Forbis is a suspenseful and driving story with tension you feel in every part of your body. The story, the characterization, the writing itself—I love everything about this book.

Wil Forbis's writing style is exquisite. The attention to detail without overwriting is magnificent and refreshing. The powerful wording and the way things occur and unfold in the story speak not only to skill but true writing talent. This is a sensory reading experience you see, feel, and even smell—and with this being in the horror genre, that can be quite uncomfortable. The characters are vivid, provocative, and very engaging. They will have you cringing, laughing out loud, scowling, and smirking knowingly.

Extra kudos for a very human but strong female protagonist. Lisa is presented as a realistic and believable character. She is flawed but not overdramatic, strong without being cold or overblown. I felt for her, felt with her, shook my head at her perception and choices, and rooted for her when she leaned toward what I approved of. I found all of the characters thus engaging; some, however, I wanted to kick in the proverbial jewels.

I cannot say enough good things about this incredible novel. It has elements of psychological horror, supernatural horror, and suspense—so much suspense and tension. *What Waits in the Shadows* is a shelf-worthy, 5-star, highly recommended chilling horror read that will have you side-eying dark shadows for days to come. I look forward to reading more from this talented new author.

Available in Kindle and Paperback on Amazon.

About the Author: Wil Forbis

Wil Forbis is an author of horror and suspense fiction that simmers with tension before exploding into action. His short stories have been featured in horror anthologies, and his novel "What Waits in the Shadows" was released in January 2024. "Anonymous," a twist on the classic masked slasher premise, will follow.

Wil was born in Montana, grew up in Hawaii, and has lived in many cities on the west coast of the United States. In addition to writing, he is a professional musician.

Until next time,

Lisa Lee Tone

SANGUIVORE

Let Creeper's Newest Album Creep Up on You

By Lucius Valiant

I'd never heard of Creeper before I went to Alice Cooper's London show in 2022, where they were the appetizer. As soon as the chorus of "Annabelle"—probably the most earworm-inducing and hard-hitting single off the band's 2020 album, *Sex, Death & the Infinite Void*—reverberated through the O2 Arena, I knew that this band had something.

I'm not stating this lightly. I'm an astrologically challenged Earth sign; I need a new band placed in front of me on about seven different occasions before I finally start paying any attention, and I add a new band or a new album to my list of favorites only with great reluctance and after careful deliberation. To get on my playlist is about as difficult and strenuous a process as becoming the next pope.

If it hadn't taken me about a century to warm to a new band, I would have gotten on board with Creeper sooner. For the past few years, friends who know my fondness for dark, gothic, theatrical rock have been recommending Creeper to me, independently of each other and with increasing frequency. I'm also sure that I must have heard some of their music played, but for whatever reason, it took Creeper getting up on stage and playing "Annabelle" at the O2 Arena before I was convinced.

Since then, Creeper has not let me down on my assumption. As the band's latest musical offering, *Sanguivore*, triumphantly proves, this band is plugged in to that magical realm that dreams, nightmares, visions, and all the best art comes from.

SANGUIVORE

Sanguivore is Creeper's third studio album, released on 13 October 2023 on Spinefarm Records. It is the worthy heir to the UK rockers' first two albums, *Eternity, In Your Arms* (2017) and *Sex, Death & the Infinite Void* (2020).

Like its two predecessors, *Sanguivore* is dark, theatrical, and packed with pain, beauty, adrenaline, and intriguing storylines.

But the distinguishing factor that sets *Sanguivore* apart and places it in a league above the others is the victorious dexterity of its execution. There's something deeply inspiring about seeing the trajectory of an artist or a band from early promise to potential in full bloom. That's what's happening with Creeper on *Sanguivore*, where everything from vocalist Will Gould's impressively versatile vocals to the all-out, Meat Loaf-esque theatricality of the compositions seems to reach new heights. The result is, for want of a better word, banging.

As a writer of vampire fiction, I admittedly have some extra love for *Sanguivore*, since it is an album telling a story (or rather, several stories) about vampires and immortality. According to an interview the band gave with *Rolling Stone*, the album was inspired by the COVID-19 lockdown in the United Kingdom and the subsequent return of live music. On the album, this return to life, to art, and to music becomes the story of a vampiric resurrection.

The album features ten tracks, opening with "Further Than Forever" and closing with "More Than Death."

"Further Than Forever" is over nine minutes long and starts like the soundtrack of a movie that doesn't exist but very much should. As the thunderclouds and guitar riffs roll in, you almost cannot help but visualize the opening credits rolling across your vision in bright red gothic font.

I would struggle to pick one favorite song off *Sanguivore*, but if someone were to hold a gun to my head and demand a choice, I might go with "Cry to Heaven." The album's second track is hard-hitting, intense, and unapologetically catchy. It's the kind of gothic '80s-inspired rock song you can listen to again and again without getting tired of it. "Cry to Heaven" has it all—a catchy melody, memorable lyrics (revolving around blood lust and damnation), driving guitars, and a big chorus that sweeps you along in a reverie. If you're a Sisters of Mercy fan, you'll love this one. "Cry to Heaven" is also a great example of Will Gould's vocal versatility, as he leans into the darker, deeper end of his register.

"Sacred Blasphemy," the third track on *Sanguivore*, is short, intense, and heavier than most other Creeper songs to date, followed and contrasted by "The Ballad of Spook & Mercy," a track in a much slower tempo, with stripped-back guitars, a drum that effectively works as the song's heartbeat, and haunting, ethereal female backing vocals. "The Ballad of Spook & Mercy" is a short story in song form, relaying the story of the vampire girl Mercy, who awakens beneath the honeymoon to attack a newlywed couple in a parked Corvette.

Next up is "Lovers Led Astray," another album favorite of mine. Like "Cry to Heaven," this one is a gothic rock song that brings to mind something the Sisters of Mercy might have recorded in the '80s and forgotten to release. It's dark and seductive, its intensity fabulously contrasted by the deliberate pauses and gaps that seem to create the effect of held breaths throughout the song. The tempo changes and interesting choral arrangements only make this dark, sexy ballad all the more listenable.

British rock band Creeper onstage at the O2 Academy, Bristol on 5 November 2023. Photo Credit Andre666

The best way I can think of describing "Teenage Sacrifice" is as a guitar-driven track with a catchy chorus that brings to mind rolling thunder clouds above a cemetery at night while a group of robe-clad figures gather in preparation for an unspeakable ritual.

Then we have "Chapel Gates." In this song, Creeper's post-punk influences and origins bleed through into the otherwise more polished sound the band has grown into. It's a welcome reappearance of an earlier sound, almost like an homage to an earlier version of the band and to its history. The track is short, punchy, and upbeat, delivering us to the opening bars of "The Abyss," the album's only instrumental track, featuring both organ and those marvelous rolling thunderclouds, for a short breather before "Black Heaven" sweeps us away with its dark, distorted, more futuristic vibe. Indeed, you can never accuse Creeper of being afraid of experimenting and reinventing their sound. This willingness to experiment might not be everyone's cup of tea, but it's one of the things I have come to really appreciate about the band.

The last track on *Sanguivore* is "More Than Death," a rock ballad that Meat Loaf would have been proud to call his own. This track is slower and more emotional than any other on the album, which gives it a redemptive, epilogue-esque quality; a satisfying ending to the various stories that the album tells.

If you are a fan of the Sisters of Mercy, Alice Cooper, My Chemical Romance, or Meat Loaf, or if you are simply wondering where the next Alice Cooper is hiding among the millennial generation, do yourself a favor and give Creeper a listen. Start with *Sanguivore* and work your way backwards. You will find gems from throughout the band's musical history, though I'd venture a guess that *Sanguivore* is going to hit you the hardest. This album just simply nails what it attempts to do.

Sanguivore track listing

No. Title   Length

1. "Further Than Forever" 9:12

2. "Cry to Heaven" 4:27

3. "Sacred Blasphemy"   2:53

4. "The Ballad of Spook & Mercy"   4:39

5. "Lovers Led Astray"   4:40

6. "Teenage Sacrifice"   4:17

7. "Chapel Gates" 2:23

8. "The Abyss"   0:42

9. "Black Heaven" 4:15

10. "More Than Death"   4:38

Total length: 42:06

Special edition bonus tracks

No. Title   Writer(s)   Length

11. "Shadows of the Night" (Pat Benatar Cover) David Leigh Byron, Rachel Sweet 4:03

12. "Love And Pain"   4:13

13. "Phantom Fantasia"   3:07

14. "Cry to Heaven - Count Dalgula's Queen Of The Night Extended Mix"   5:27

Total length: 58:56

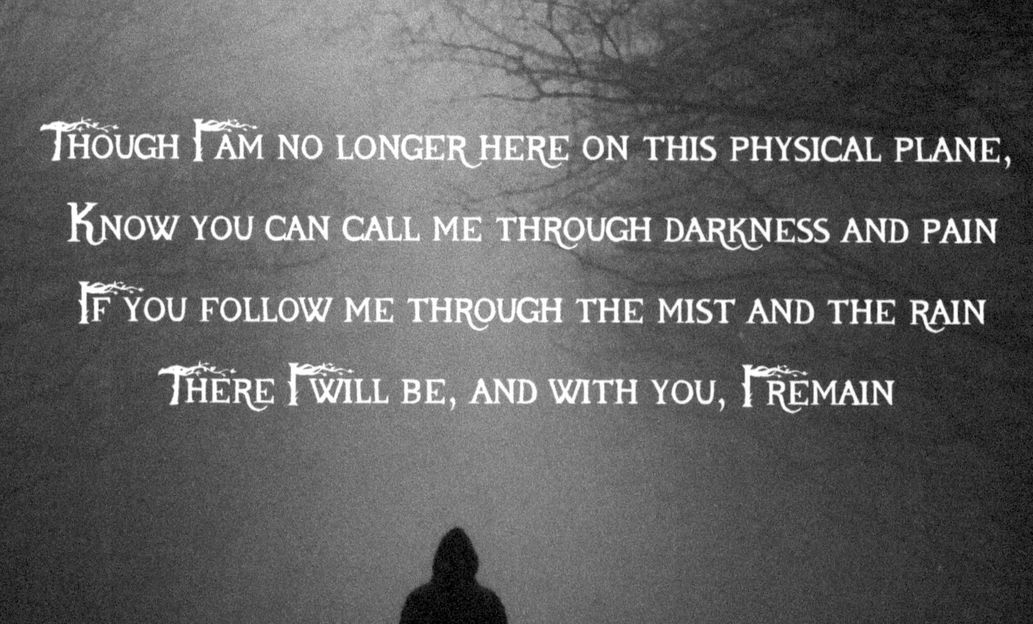

Though I am no longer here on this physical plane,
Know you can call me through darkness and pain
If you follow me through the mist and the rain
There I will be, and with you, I remain

YOU SHOULD BE WRITING:IN MEMORY OF JAMES A. MOORE

By Thomas R. Clark

I'm well read. Since I was a young man, I have always found solace in the words of others. It's no surprise that I, too, evolved from being a reader to a creator—how could I not with all of the stories I've lost myself in over the decades? My path as a writer has been on a road paved with the imaginations of too many creatives to count. Each of them has made an impact on me, some more than others, but regardless, I am the sum of all that I have consumed or have been fortunate enough to be associated with. And this leads us to the memorial at hand.

In 2015, I was offered an opportunity to engineer and mix the *Three Guys with Beards* podcast, hosted by a trio of creative fiction heavy hitters in Christopher Golden, Jonathan Mayberry, and one James A. Moore. I'd long adored the work of these men, and having been given this opportunity, I accepted the challenge with gusto! I became the fourth beard, behind the scenes. And though I didn't contribute to the content, I was educated by it. Of the trio, I knew Moore's name well, more prominently from nearly 30 years previous.

My first introduction to James A. Moore was his work with White Wolf Games and the World of Darkness. His input on this game impacted me a great deal as a horror fan and now as a creator. You see, I learned much about world building from not only the likes of Robert E. Howard and Stephen King but also from the World of Darkness. In particular, Jim Moore's contributions to the game resonated with me. From wild west werewolves to vampires lurking in the shadows of the dark ages, from the seedy underbelly of Berlin's nightlife to the necropolis we call Atlanta, I found myself enamored. Moore taught me how to blend reality and fantasy into something Middle America could suspend disbelief for.

Imagine my shock when I was handed the responsibility of editing this man's podcast a quarter century later. During this time, and continuing after the suspension of *Three Guys with Beards*, I got to know him a little. I can't say he and I were friends, albeit we were friendly with one another. Adult-me got the chance on multiple occasions to pick this sage's mind at events such as NECON and Scares That Care. I learned of his boisterous approach to getting the work done. Comments like "Ass in chair, fingers on keys" or "You should be writing" come to mind. How about the T-shirt going around right now, where Jim declares "GET OUT OF MY FACE AND FINISH YOUR MANUSCRIPT!"

Ever the hippy with a mop of hair and a wild beard, James A. Moore personified what it meant to be a creator and writer. He was as generous with his compassion as he was prolific with his writing. And man, oh man, could he ever hug you. It was a bear hug

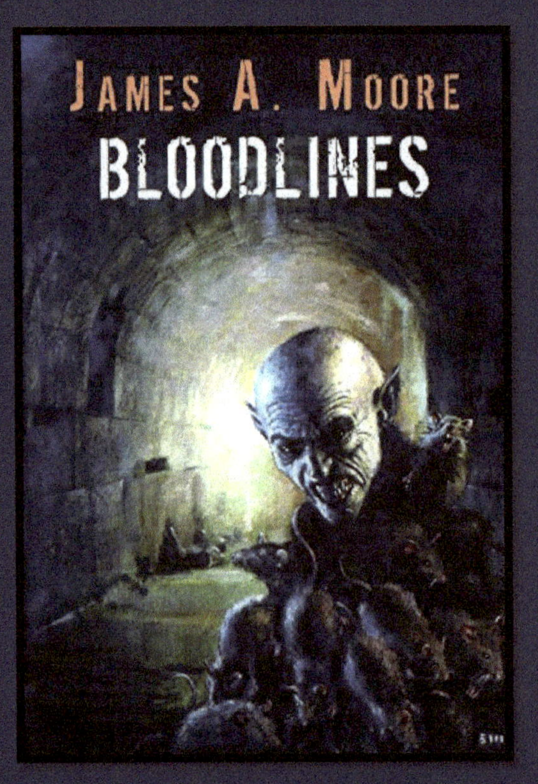

supersized professional wrestlers would be envious of. But instead of making you pass out, it filled you with elation and oxytocin. Much like the aforementioned Robert E. Howard, he may have resembled any number of the anti-heroes or ruffians in his fiction, but James A. Moore was a kind man with empathy and compassion. I'm happy to say I've been the recipient of this generous man's affection on more than one occasion.

Last year at NECON, James gave me one of those signature hugs and told me how proud he was of me for accomplishing what I have in such a small amount of time. This affirmation of my art from a man who inspired me sent shivers down my spine. Recently, one of his peers from the White Wolf days informed me how my writing reminded them of Jim's writing from that era. I couldn't have been more honored to accept the compliment. You see, Jim Moore wrote, and he wrote like a fucking beast, so getting compared to him was at once invigorating and humbling. Jim released dozens upon dozens of novels and hundreds of short stories throughout his long career.

Over the last couple years, since the cancer struck, I got to know Jim a little and learned some of his history. Outside of his writing, as it is with all of us, James A. Moore's life had its ups and downs. In particular, how his previous wife passed and how he reconnected with his first love decades later. This second chance became bittersweet, as life is often unkind and unfair and will sucker punch you without a care. You see, not long after remarrying, James woke up one morning with a substantial tumor on his neck. Intrepid doctors were able to save him, but at a severe cost. The treatment to save his life did as much damage as the cancer, and ultimately, it became too much for his body to take. James A. Moore passed away on March 27, 2024. He was 58 years old.

James A. Moore's best friend was Christopher Golden, and it's through Chris that many of us in the horror community learned of Jim's passing. We all would be blessed to have such a friend as Chris was to Jim. I think Chris will understand when I sum this up with a paraphrasing of Jim's heartfelt words of encouragement to both aspiring and long-term writers:

"You should be writing; get your face out of this magazine!"

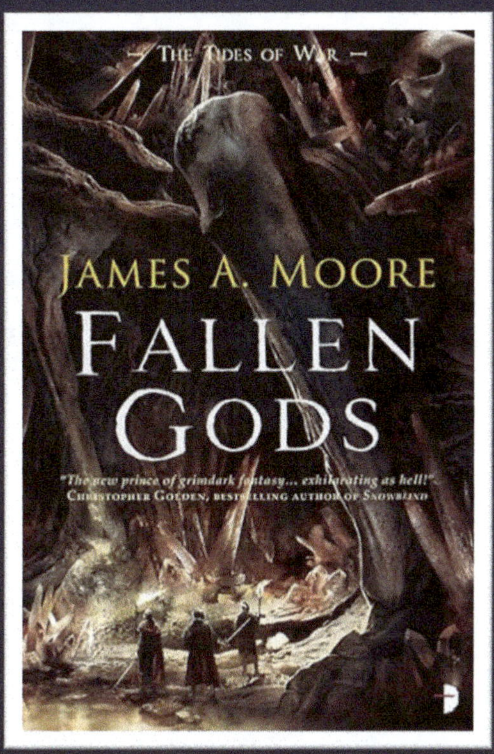

JAMES A. MOORE

BY D. PARDEE WHITING

I first met James A. Moore at Scares That Care in 2018 and was amazed at how warm and friendly he was. He took the time to chat and share his thoughts on writing and editing, and I felt as if I found a kindred spirit. So when Lisa Vasquez started *House of Stitched Magazine* a few years ago, I jumped at the opportunity to interview Moore. With Moore's passing, I felt the pull to reintroduce readers to the prolific author. The following is an excerpt from that original interview, which can be found in the first issue of *HOS*.

(James A.) Moore is the author of many different books across genres. In addition to his horror books and many short stories in anthologies like in Jonathan Maberry's *V-Wars* series, a book in the *Alien* series, *The Haunted Forest Tour* he co-wrote with Jeff Strand, *Seven Forges* series, and the books *Blind Shadows* and *Congregations of the Dead* he wrote with his good friend Charles R. Rutledge, he also did a lot of work for White Wolf Games.

Moore, who is "fond of writing," first started out wanting to be a comic book artist, until he realized he "had no talent for drawing, but I had some people tell me I was telling a really good story and I should try writing. So finally, I broke down and tried it."

This, he said, was when he was 22 or 23 years old. "I never went to college. Couldn't afford it."

Moore's interest in comic books came at young age, he said, adding he would read them pretty much nonstop when he was growing up.

All through his school age years, Moore's family would move around a lot, so he wound up with 12 years of education at 17 different schools.

"Dad was out of the picture. Mom was doing her best with six kids," he said. "Back in the seventies, it wasn't so easy for a woman to be an executive anything. She was an executive housekeeper, and we would go where the money was."

Moore said after starting out in Georgia, he's lived in Colorado, California, Maryland, Louisiana, and then back to Georgia. With all the moving around during his school years, Moore didn't make friends. "I read comic books instead."

Unfortunately, or fortunately, depending on how you look at it, this led to bullying. He said he was bullied a lot. He added he learned how to run faster.

Some authors write their school bullies into their work as a way to get a form of payback; however, Moore said he didn't want to remember them. He would rather leave them in the past, write, and enjoy his life.

Although Moore began building an impressive list of successful works of fiction with *Under the Overtree* when he was 23, followed the next year by *House of Secrets* with Kevin P. Murphy, his very first foray into writing happened when he was 14.

"Around the age of 14, I tried writing a novel," the author said. "I got 350 pages in before I realized it had no plot. Spent an entire summer typing away." Despite being therapeutic, he said, "It wasn't very good, so I threw it out. I still have pieces I can yank out if I wanted to. I just haven't."

Moore's success comes from writing whatever strikes his fancy. "I don't like being told what I can and can't write."

The 55-year-old (at the time of this writing) author likes to do things his own way, which includes sometimes using familiar creatures; however, he prefers trying to create his own critters for his stories. According to Moore, it's all been done; it's just a matter of doing it his way.

Even though he does like to do things his way, Moore is not above having strong editors. For people who ask if they really need an editor and can't they just publish themselves, he said, "Yes, you need an editor; yes, you can publish it yourself. Just don't be stupid about it."

Bad editing annoys him, he said, adding taking shortcuts you shouldn't take is not a good idea. "For lack of a better way to put it, unless you give it six months, you're not going to see the mistakes you've made. You'll paint right over them. So either take six months away from the project or have somebody else edit it or both." Preferably both.

When he worked with White Wolf Games, they had rules to follow. "One of their big rules is 'Let's try to avoid redundancies'." Moore explains this got him in the habit of never using the same word within three pages. "I love words. I think they are glorious. I love names for the same reason." Because of this love of words and names, Moore collects them. "I may never use them, but I collect them."

Another of Moore's way includes writing every day, oftentimes with music playing. What type of music will vary, but normally, he said, he will choose classic '70s; although, he has also listened to horror movie scores on more than one occasion. In reality, though, just like switching around what he writes, he also switches around what he listens to based on what he is working on at the time.

"I'll listen to a lot of instrumental music scores when I'm doing the Seven Forges stuff. But, for example, I did a young adult series, and on that, I was mostly listening to the *Sopranos* soundtrack. It was never even consciously. It's just background noise."

However, he admitted most often he will listen to music before he sits down and writes than when actually writing. Sometimes, though, music does not help get the words on the page.

CAMP MEMENTO MORI...
ZZZZZ
RAWRG...
ZZZZ...
RAWRG...
ARGHHH!
FINALLY!
YES!
RARRGH??
I HAVE BEEN WAITING ALL SUMMER FOR THIS!
WHAT'S IT GONNA BE BIG GUY?
LET'S DO THIS!
OLD FASHIONED SLASHING? BLUNT FORCE TRAUMA?
POP MY EYES OUTTA MY SKULL WITH YOUR BARE HANDS?
ARHHG?
NO WAY!
SCARED?
I'M NOT SCARED...

YOU GOTTA BE KIDDING...
INFLATION IS OUT OF CONTROL, WE'RE CONSTANTLY ON THE VERGE OF WWIII, TIKTOK IS ROTTING THE BRAINS OF MY ENTIRE GENERATION, HOMELESSNESS IS AT A 40 YEAR HIGH, RENEWABLE ENERGY IS AN EMPTY PIPE DREAM CONSTANTLY BEING BLOCKED BY CORRUPT CORPORATIONS AND THEIR LOBBYISTS, THE ONLY PEOPLE RUNNING FOR PRESIDENT MAY HAVE ATTENDED LINCOLN'S INAUGURATION, BIRD FLU IS MAKING A COMEBACK, THE TESLA CYBER TRUCK IS AN ACTUAL THING AND MAD MAX FURIOSA FLOPPED AT THE BOX OFFICE.
???
ONLY THING THAT SCARES ME IS SPENDING ANOTHER 60 YEARS ON THIS PLANET!
SO COME ON BUDDY... TAKE ME OUT!
RARRGH
SWEET RELEASE OF DEATH!
RARGHH
YOU'RE SUPPOSED TO KILL ME!
I WANT A SUCKING CHEST WOUND!!!
HEY!
THIS FEELS LIKE A HUG!
I DON'T WANT A DAMN HUG!
SEE YA NEXT TIME - KABLAMM

PLEASE CHECK OUT THE FLASH
FICTION FROM THE WINNING
PARTICIPANTS OF OUR
FACEBOOK SLASH FLASH
CONTEST!

BELLE MANOR

By Patric Mauzy

Tarnished now were the boards that had built Belle Manor, that hellish house hidden back in a tangle of crooked trees that Ben Belle's father had built for his mother back in the 70's, and as Ben walked up the lonely driveway toward the house all of his suppressed emotions from the past came flooding back into him. The thrashings, the scoldings, the isolation. His fists clenched tightly as a resurgence of hatred coursed through his veins, and he couldn't help but smile at the thought of what was to become of the house now that his parents were dead and gone, and the ownership of the house had transferred over to him.

This is the last time I'll ever see it, he thought, looking up toward the empty house. There was a light burning on the front porch, and it cast a dim orange glow out into the darkness. Tomorrow they'll knock it down, and there'll be nothing left but dust to scatter into the wind. Good riddance.

As he stood there looking at the old house, something caught his eye; a flicker of movement in the window beside the front door. But that was impossible. No one should be in there, he thought, moving toward the porch steps. The movers finished up this afternoon. The place should be empty.

He was halfway up the stairs when the front door swung open, and out stepped his father, alive and looking well.

"Welcome home, sonny boy!" his father said. "Did you miss your old man?"

"You're not real," Ben said, taking a nervous step back. "You can't be real."

His father shrugged. "I'm real enough. Real enough to be standing here talking to you at least."

"But . . . you died," Ben said slowly. "The car . . . mom . . . you . . . mangled."

"Yeah," his father said with a laugh. "Definitely not the best turn I ever made, but oh well. What can ya do, am I right? Anyway, I don't got a lot of time here, but I just had to swing by and say that if you tear down my house tomorrow, no, put one finger on my house tomorrow . . ." He came down the steps at a speed Ben had never seen his father move, and placed a surprisingly strong hand on Ben's shoulder. "I will personally come back and find you, and drag you down to hell myself. Capisce?"

"Capisce," Ben mumbled, gulping. "Loud and clear."

"Good," his father said, grinning, and for a moment Ben thought his eyes turned a bright shade of red (it was probably only his imagination, he told himself later). "I'll tell your mother you said hi!"

And then he was gone, like dust in the wind.

Ben stood there staring up at the house a moment longer, and then turned back toward the driveway and made a mad dash for his car, screaming the whole way

HOUSE OF HUNGER

By Shane Ford

Alex hated clichés. As if breaking down on a deserted highway in the middle of the night wasn't bad enough, now he and his girlfriend Mads had to walk through the woods in hopes of finding someone to help them out. Alex switched on the flashlight he pulled from his backpack.

"Let's get this show on the road", he said to Mads as they crossed the forest edge.

After what felt like an hour of walking through the wet and humid forest, they felt a glimmer of hope.

In front of them a house stood eerily still, while the moon cast a dark silhouette of the massive abode onto the ground in front of them. In the windows they could see a faint light pulsing in the rhythm of their heartbeats.

They stepped onto the porch. The old wood creaking beneath them as Alex reached out to knock on the door.

The door opened under the weight of Alex's knock. Almost as if it had been left ajar.

As they crossed the threshold, the door slammed shut behind them, and the couple found themselves in a grand hall adorned with portraits that seemed to watch their every move. The air was thick with the scent of decay, and the sound of their footsteps echoed as if the house itself was listening.

Mads felt a chill run down her spine. She flashed a terrified look to Alex, which he returned in kind.

They tried to leave, but the door refused to budge. The windows were sealed shut, and the portraits' eyes followed them, filled with looks of terror. The house was toying with them, a cat with its mice.

As the night progressed, the true horror began. The couple heard whispers emanating from the walls, voices begging for release, for salvation. They realized then that the house was not just a structure; it was a predator, and they were the prey.

The floors groaned beneath them, wooden planks curling like fingers trying to grasp at their feet. The house was hungry, and it had set the table for its feast.

In a desperate bid for escape, Mads and Alex split up, searching for an exit. But the house was a labyrinth. They were inside the belly of the beast, and it was digesting them slowly, savoring its meal.

Mads found herself in a room with no doors, the walls closing in on her. She screamed for Alex, but her voice was swallowed by the house. The last thing she saw was the wallpaper peeling back to reveal a toothy, gaping maw, and she was consumed by the darkness.

Alex ran towards the screams, only to find himself in the same room Mads had been in. He could hear breathing all around him, the walls pulsing with every step he took.

As the floor swallowed him whole, his final scream echoed through the forest. Not a soul to hear it. Except the ones in the house. They would never leave.

THE HOUSE JACK BUILT

By Kim Mixon Hill

Jack hadn't been to his childhood home in a few months, but he saw the welcoming light as he walked the makeshift road, surrounded by woods. It was a brisk September, and the leaves had started to change. Even though it was night, the full moon lit up the path.

As he got closer, he thought about all the horrors of growing up in that house. An abusive father, a mother who turned a blind eye, and his "perfect" sister who never took the brunt of anyone's wrath. Not even his.

He'd changed, though. He'd moved out, moved on, and established himself as someone others looked up to. "Jack tick, Jack tick," he thought, as he walked. While he eventually got out, he still had his little tics, and saying his own name with random words was one of them. But the tics kept him grounded. He knew he was special, it just took some time to figure things out.

He remembered how his father would come home, smelling of sour whiskey and cigarettes. And how he'd take the beatings - time after time. Telling his mother was pointless. She'd seen it with her own eyes, and simply say, "Jacky, why do you antagonize him? It's your fault." His sister Rebecca was worthless. She was pleased it wasn't her that was being punched around.

The day before he moved out, she'd cried out, saying that she suffered too. But Jack knew that she was probably making that up. Anything to get her way, he thought. His mother had begged and pleaded with him, but he was dead set on leaving the way he wanted to. And he held nothing back. Even as his father tried to get the better of him, Jack was steadfast and surprised by his own solidity. In the end, he got his way, and left his home behind.

Now it was time to return and take care of some business. As he unlocked the door, he first saw Rebecca. Still so pretty and young, sitting in the living room recliner. His dad was in the kitchen, at the table, with a bottle of whiskey and a pack of Marlboros. Lastly, he found his mother in the cellar.

In fact, everyone was just how he'd left them. His father with the broken bottle shoved into his mouth. His mother chained in the cellar, where he left her to starve. And Rebecca with her throat cut - flaxen hair almost as beautiful as it was when he lived there. Everyone had tried to reason with him. They even tried to blame him. His advances on his sister. The fights with his dad over it. And his mom begging him to get help.

This was better. He could finally live in peace.

SUBURBAN SCHIZOPHRENIA SIMULACRUM

By Eric M. Esquivel

The Internet called Sebas a "serial arsonist", but that wasn't true at all. He hadn't "burned down multiple homes, while the innocent tenants slept inside", like they said on Facebook.

For starters: All of the houses that Seb had laid waste to were all the same home. He didn't know why...Sebastian wasn't a scientist...But he was sure of it nonetheless. Absolute, and without a doubt. The way people say you're sure when you meet the one you're gonna marry, or sure when you pass a bunch of giggling teenagers in a pharmacy parking lot and you just know—deep in your bones, where God keeps The Truth at— that it's you that they were laughing at.

Even if some of the homes' regenerations got some of the details wrong (like the color, the shape, and/or the size, for instance) they all still felt like the one that Sebas had grown up in the shadow of. And that was infinitely more important. Because any asshole with a Home Depot Rewards Card could emulate the sickly shade of avocado green that the two-story terror was when Seb first encountered it. Small details like that were neither here nor there. But that feeling, the falling-in-a-dream / belly-full-of-gas-station-sushi dull ache in the gut that sprouted in his lower intestines whenever he looked up at it? That was a singular feeling that could not be faked. And it was real— despite what any therapists, or Internet forum know-it-alls wanted to claim.

And the people inside these houses, the ones who burned along with them? They were far from innocent. How could they be? Walking through an embodiment of pure evil like that and allowing its dust into their lungs, its splinters beneath their skin, its telepathically blasted thoughts into their sleeping minds.

They had to burn. They all had to burn. And Sebas was just the only man righteous enough to step up and get the damn thing done.

It was his calling. And he had started young. The head shrinkers called Seb's earliest work of exorcism-by-flame an "act of misplaced aggression", claiming that he somehow got his wires crossed because of the profound emotional and physical damage that he was subjected to in his neighbors' attic when he went missing for those three days that he still—to this day, at 24 years old— can only remember in violent flashes of red light and the piercing sound of someone (or something?) using his own voice to scream. That him blaming the "supernatural" house for what was done to him instead of the commonly-evil people who resided within it was some kind of gentle mercy from Sebastian's trauma-addled brain.

Doctors were goofy. Seb knew how the world worked. He knew what had to be done. And, he thought to himself as he struck the last match in his decades-old matchbook, he knew just how to do it

We thank everyone who participated and hope to see many more stories from our readers and fans!

Please note, these stories are raw and unedited. We kept them in their original format to preserve the way they were submitted for votes.

These are readers and fans favorites, and we had no part in the choosing of these stories.

Congratulations to all the winners!

--Memento Mori Staff

www.facebook.com/mementomoriinkmag

House of Stitched Magazine undergoes a transformative rebranding under the leadership of Lisa Vasquez, who assumes the role of Editor-in-Chief once more, creating a new era for the publication as Memento Mori Ink Magazine.

With over ten years in the horror genre and having established herself in the community through her work at House of Stitched and Stitched Smile Publications, Vasquez brings her unique vision to Memento Mori Ink.

The rebranding effort represents a strategic alignment with Crystal Lake Entertainment, a collaboration aimed at elevating the voices of indie artists across various mediums. This partnership between Vasquez and Crystal Lake Entertainment's CEO, Joe Mynhardt, combines their dedication to providing a platform for emerging authors and elevating the indie arts scene.

As an accomplished author, publisher, and mentor, Vasquez's influence extends beyond the pages of Memento Mori Ink. Her commitment to nurturing new authors within the horror community has earned her recognition and respect among her peers. She advocates for the promotion and support of artists and authors from diverse backgrounds, including women, LGBTQ+ individuals, and individuals from various ethnic and cultural backgrounds.

It was a well-timed decision for Joe, who wanted to expand the Crystal Lake catalog to include a magazine. But the opportunity hadn't yet presented itself, until Lisa. Knowing a magazine requires passion, talent, knowledge, care, and feeding, Joe recognized those qualities in Lisa Vasquez. He also saw something essential—leadership. "As an ambassador for creative minds, I'm excited to unleash Memento Mori Ink under Lisa's leadership," Joe said. "Her passion for storytelling and dedication to nurturing talent make her an invaluable asset to the literary community. I'm proud to be a part of this journey and eager to see the magazine thrive."

CRYSTAL LAKE MISSION STATEMENT

Since its founding in August 2012, Crystal Lake Publishing has quickly become one of the world's leading publishers of Dark Fiction and Horror books. In 2023, Crystal Lake Publishing formed a part of Crystal Lake Entertainment, joining several other divisions, including Torrid Waters, Crystal Lake Comics, and many more.

While we strive to present only the highest quality fiction and entertainment, we also endeavour to support authors along their writing journey. We offer our time and experience in non-fiction projects, as well as author mentoring and services, at competitive prices.

With several Bram Stoker Award wins and many other wins and nominations (including the HWA's Specialty Press Award), Crystal Lake puts integrity, honor, and respect at the forefront of our publishing operations.

We strive for each book and outreach program we spearhead to not only entertain and touch or comment on issues that affect our readers, but also to strengthen and support the Dark Fiction field and its authors.

Not only do we find and publish authors we believe are destined for greatness, but we strive to work with men and women who endeavour to be decent human beings who care more for others than themselves, while still being hard-working, driven, and passionate artists and storytellers.

Crystal Lake is and will always be a beacon of what passion and dedication, combined with overwhelming teamwork and respect, can accomplish. We endeavour to know each and every one of our readers, while building personal relationships with our authors, reviewers, bloggers, podcasters, bookstores, and libraries.

We will be as trustworthy, forthright, and transparent as any business can be, while also keeping most of the headaches away from our authors, since it's our job to solve the problems so they can stay in a creative mind. Which of course also means paying our authors.

We do not just publish books, we present to you worlds within your world, doors within your mind, from talented authors who sacrifice so much for a moment of your time.

There are some amazing small presses out there, and through collaboration and open forums we will continue to support other presses in the goal of helping authors and showing the world what quality small presses are capable of accomplishing. No one wins when a small press goes down, so we will always be there to support hardworking, legitimate presses and their authors. We don't see Crystal Lake as the best press out there, but we will always strive to be the best, strive to be the most interactive and grateful, and even blessed press around. No matter what happens over time, we will also take our mission very seriously while appreciating where we are and enjoying the journey.

What do we offer our authors that they can't do for themselves through self-publishing?

We are big supporters of self-publishing (especially hybrid publishing), if done with care, patience, and planning. However, not every author has the time or inclination to do market research, advertise, and set up book launch strategies. Although a lot of authors are successful in doing it all, strong small presses will always be there for the authors who just want to do what they do best: write.

What we offer is experience, industry knowledge, contacts and trust built up over years. And due to our strong brand and trusting fanbase, every Crystal Lake book comes with weight of respect. In time our fans begin to trust our judgment and will try a new author purely based on our support of said author.

To date we've published around 100 books, and with each launch we strive to fine-tune our approach, learn from our mistakes, and increase our reach. We continue to assure our authors that we're here for them and that we'll carry the weight of the launch and deal with third parties while they focus on their strengths—be it writing, interviews, blogs, signings, etc.

We also offer several mentoring packages to authors that include knowledge and skills they can use in both traditional and self-publishing endeavors.

We look forward to launching many new careers.

This is what we believe in. What we stand for. This will be our legacy.

Welcome to CRYSTAL LAKE ENTERTAINMENT.

"Crystal Lake are good people doing fine work. Always worth watching for their latest."

Jack Ketchum, The Girl Next Door and Off-Season

"One look at Crystal Lake's track record (as well as the stellar titles in their forthcoming lineup) and you know they're the real deal. CLP are here to stay and for the ultimate horror fan, that's a reason to rejoice!"

Kealan Patrick Burke, Bram Stoker Award-winning author of The Turtle Boy, Kin, and Sour Candy

www.ingramcontent.com/pod-product-compliance
Lightning Source LLC
Chambersburg PA
CBHW041141300726
48978CB00016B/1336